Faith and Hope

Amy R Anguish

MANTLE ROCK
PUBLISHING LLC
MantleRockPublishingLLC.com

©2019 by Amy Anguish

Published by Mantle Rock Publishing LLC
2879 Palma Road
Benton, KY 42025
http://mantlerockpublishingllc.com

Printed in the United States of America

All rights reserved. No part of this publication may be reproduced, stored in a retrieval system, or transmitted in any form or by any means—for example, electronic, photocopy and recording— without the prior written permission of the publisher. The only exception is brief quotation in printed reviews.

ISBN 978-1-945094-82-8

Cover by Diane Turpin at dianeturpindesigns.com

All characters are fictional, and any resemblance to real people, either factional or historical, is purely coincidental.

Scripture taken from the New King James Version®. Copyright © 1982 by Thomas Nelson. Used by permission. All rights reserved.

This year, I want to dedicate this book to my husband, Jeremy Anguish, the love of my life, who has gone through a lot with me over our marriage. I love him more than I thought I could love another person, and I thank God every day for giving me a helpmate and supporter and friend. Thank you for loving me back and believing in me, Jeremy.

CHAPTER 1

HOPE

"In all honesty, I really thought this meeting might have been to say I was going to get a raise next year." Hope Cook gave a little chuckle. Anything was better than bursting into tears in front of her boss, even if it was faking laughter.

"Trust me, Hope. If I could have done that, you would be at the top of my list." Mr. Smith straightened some papers. "Unfortunately, the school board has spoken. The team has to have another coach."

"I know." Hope half-heartedly held up a fist. "Go Buckley!"

"If anything changes at all, I'll let you know."

Hope couldn't help but slump her shoulders as she opened the doors to rain. Evidently, the weather was in the same mood she was. She stepped out from under the overhang ... and directly into a puddle.

Laid off.

Wet clothes.

Soaked feet.

She listed every bad thing the afternoon had wrought thus far as she squished her way through the parking lot.

"You have got to be kidding me." The umbrella doused her with another shower as she fought to close it. She tossed the miscreant tool into her backseat and slammed the door.

She took a moment to lay her head on the steering wheel and give in to her depression. "Why, God? Why give me my dream job only to take it away?"

A clap of thunder sounded. She lifted her head and hands.

"Okay, okay. Sorry. But I don't understand."

She shook her head. Was she really arguing with God? Obviously, she needed to go home and rest.

Her mother's ringtone jingled as Hope cranked the engine. She slid the car into gear and answered the call.

"Hi, honey. Can you talk?"

"Sure." Hope propped the phone between her head and shoulder.

"You sound down." Mom had always been able to tell how her daughters were doing just by listening to their tones of voice—even when they tried to hide it.

"It's been a rough day." Hope checked her mirrors. "Mr. Smith told me they don't have a position for me in the fall. They need a coach, and since coaches usually teach math, and I was the last hired …"

"Oh, Hope." Mom sighed. "What will you do?"

Hope made a careful right turn and avoided most of the puddle that covered half the intersection. Her wipers swished against the onslaught of water that covered her windshield anyway. "Not sure yet. I mean, there's more than one high school in Oxford. Surely one of them needs a math teacher. And Mr. Smith promised me a letter of recommendation."

Perhaps if Hope kept thinking positively like this, she would start believing it. More important, hopefully her mom would. When Mom got in "fix-it mode," nothing went well.

"Who knows? Maybe something will change between now and August. Buckley High might need me to come back after all."

Hope had maintained as much dignity as she could while she sat there and watched her dreams crash around her. All she had ever wanted to do was teach high school math. These last two years at Buckley had seemed like a godsend. Instead, God appeared to think she needed to look somewhere else.

She slowly maneuvered through the wet streets of Oxford and tapped her brakes as she neared a stoplight. Her car had been showing its age lately, and she didn't trust anything to work as well as it should. She slid to a stop just as the light turned green again.

"Or you could see if there's one somewhere else. I'll keep my ears open around here."

"Mom, I really don't want to live in Tennessee. No offense, but I love Mississippi."

"Hope, don't limit yourself. Maybe God wants you to move somewhere else." Mom's voice held the same note of caution and worry it had when giving advice while Hope was growing up.

"Or maybe you do." Hope ground her teeth against the desire to remind her mother that she was an adult. Her mom probably just wanted her away from Kyle, the boyfriend no one in the family seemed to approve.

She checked over her shoulder before changing to the left lane. Her last turn was coming up and she wanted to be ready in plenty of time as the rain started coming harder. She flipped her wipers to high. They beat a quick rhythm against the onslaught as hard as they could, but her visibility didn't increase much.

"Sounds loud there." Mom's voice was tinged with worry.

"It's raining, but I'm almost home."

"I should let you go until later then. You shouldn't be driving and talking on the phone at the same time, anyway."

"It's okay, Mom." Hope tapped the brakes as she neared the intersection.

"I'll call you later—" Hope didn't hear the rest of her mom's words.

The car wasn't responding. The engine was still on, the wipers still swished, but it wasn't slowing at all. She pushed the pedal harder, but nothing changed.

She dropped the phone.

"Hope? Are you okay?" Mom's voice was far away, yelling through the phone on the floor.

Both feet on the pedal now. Knuckles white on the wheel. Still nothing, and the light glared red.

She wasn't stopping. The vehicle had a mind of its own as it careened over the white line and into the intersection.

A school bus rolled through just ahead of her. She jerked her car to the left to try and avoid it, but it was too late. She closed her eyes as her sedan drifted into the back of the bus, narrowly missing the wheel.

Crunch. The sound was worse than the impact.

She slowly looked up. In the few seconds the wipers had her windshield cleared, she caught sight of several high school students staring down at her through the windows. Including two from her second level math class, ridiculously leaning from their own window to wave at her. She wasn't going to live this down anytime soon, definitely not before school let out in another couple months.

The rain covered the view again as she turned off her ignition. No one seemed hurt, but her car was wedged firmly beneath the other vehicle, and the way her hood crumpled told her she probably wouldn't be driving it again.

Just great. When I asked if this day could get any worse, it wasn't a challenge, God.

~

"Thanks for coming to get me, Cass." Hope and her best friend, Cassidy Jones, entered their apartment several hours later.

"No worries." Cassidy threw her keys on the kitchen table. The girls had been roommates since sophomore year of college. It was Cassidy who had brought Hope to Mississippi. Cass had heard about the job opening at her old high school and passed it on along with an invitation to share rent.

Hope sank into a chair and leaned her head in her hands.

"Headache?"

"In more ways than one." Hope ran her hands through her blonde hair, grimacing at the damp, tangled strands.

"Where was Kyle tonight?" Cassidy flipped her long red braid over her shoulder and began rummaging through the freezer.

"Not sure." Hope sat back up and sorted through the mail. "We were supposed to go out for dinner, but he didn't answer when I called him. Maybe his class ran long."

"When is he graduating?"

Hope made a face. "Not sure about that, either."

Kyle and Hope had been dating for almost two years now. He had changed his major three times since she met him, six times total. Her mom said he was one of those people who was going to be a professional student. He claimed he just hadn't found his niche yet.

Her phone rang, and she tossed a bill to the side. "Hello?"

"Hey, sweetheart. Are you okay?" Mom asked. "I heard the sounds of the wreck and figured I would just be in the way if I stayed on the phone."

"Yeah. Sorry I didn't call back before now. I was busy with the police report and then had to wait for Cassidy to get off work to give me a lift."

"Kyle was in class, huh?"

Hope bit down on her tongue to hold back the flippant remark about him always being in school. Just because her mom and roommate were right didn't mean she wanted to admit that to them. "Anyway, I'm okay. A little sore from the impact and the seatbelt, but somehow the airbags didn't deploy. I guess because of the angle I actually hit. More of the passenger side ended up crumpled than the driver's side. My car ..."

"Oh, Hopey." Mom used the nickname from when Hope was a child. "I'm so sorry. I feel like it was my fault for calling you then in the first place. I should have known you'd be driving home."

"You couldn't know that, Mom. I got out later than usual today because of the meeting and was going a bit slower due to the rain. I'm actually usually home by the time you called me." Hope walked back to her bedroom and slipped out of her soggy shoes.

"What can we do to help?" Mom asked.

"Not much right now. Insurance will cover at least part of it, but it's going to be totaled, I know. You can't slide under the back end of a school bus and not have totaled your car. Cassidy promised a ride to work, and I'm going to see if Kyle can pick me up. I'll work it out."

Hope smiled at the sound of her father's grumbly voice in the background. "Your father said to tell you he can come down one weekend and go car shopping if he needs to."

"Thanks. It's going to be okay, but I'll let him know if and when I go buy another vehicle."

"Hope." Mom paused, and Hope could tell something she wasn't going to like was about to come out of her mom's mouth. "I've been thinking."

"About?"

"Your job situation."

Hope let air leak through her teeth a little at a time to keep her frustration at bay.

"I know your lease comes due at the end of June. I was thinking it might make sense to get a summer job so you can have that cushion of pay ready for you in case you don't find another teaching position right away."

"Thanks for the vote of confidence, Mom." Hope flopped on her bed. "But I'll still get paid through the summer."

"Right, but if you work another job during the summer, that would be money you could put aside for later when you need it."

Hope leaned over and removed her wet socks. "What kind of job would be available for just a couple months?"

"Well, you know there's that camp your sister works at every summer …"

"Mom …"

"She might could get you a position there. You know the one? The one her friend Joe works at? And maybe she and Sam would let you stay in their spare room so you wouldn't have to pay rent. It would be good for both of you." Mom finished in a hurry.

"I'm not so sure Faith and Sam would go for that, for one thing. And for another thing, that would leave my roommate in a lurch for at least two months of having to pay all the rent herself. And for a third thing, I don't want to live in Texas, even for only two months."

"Just think about it, Hope Christine. You might even be able to find a teaching job more easily there. I think there are more jobs in Texas than just about any state right now."

"You're not listening to me." Hope closed her eyes.

"I am, too. But I know you're not taking me seriously. Think and pray about it, Hope. I'll talk to your sister and see what she thinks."

Hope hated the thought of moving in with Faith. Faith was three years older and perfect, or at least that's what it seemed like while they were growing up. Faith had planned out her life exactly how she wanted it and, so far, was fulfilling each goal. On the other hand, their mother was always trying to change Hope to be like Faith.

With this job at Buckley, things had finally been going better for her. She had her dream job, a great town to live in, a fun college team to root for, and a boyfriend who was mostly steady. Now what? Now, she was going to have to start all over again. And she didn't want to have to pick up the pieces of shattered dreams in the same house as someone whose dreams had all come true.

CHAPTER 2

FAITH

"When do you think we should tell everyone?" Sam McCreary came up behind Faith and wrapped his arms protectively around her middle, his chin resting on top of her head.

"Not yet." She put her hands over his and stared out the kitchen window. "I've always thought that spot over there would be perfect for a swing set."

Sam leaned forward to follow the direction of her finger, his stubble rough against her cheek. "I'll get right on it."

"Silly." She gave him a playful swat. "I know we won't need it for a bit, but ... but we will need it."

"Yes." He bent over and spoke to her stomach, displaying the spot on top of his head where his black hair was starting to thin. "You'll want to swing and slide as soon as you come out, won't ya, boy?"

"Boy? What if it's a she?"

"Then we'll build a swing set for her." He grabbed her hand and twirled her around. "Boy or girl, who cares? We're having a baby!"

"I still can't even believe it. After almost four years, I guess I'm still trying to wrap my mind around the fact that we're finally getting our miracle."

He pulled her back into him and kissed the side of her head. "I know. I'm just so excited I want to go shout it from the mountaintops and let the whole world know."

She laughed. "Our moms would never forgive us if we told the whole world before them."

"So, when are we going to tell the moms?"

"I was thinking Mother's Day." She turned around to face him. "That gives us not quite a month to enjoy it for ourselves ... and make sure nothing goes wrong—"

"Nothing's going to go wrong!"

She spread her fingers over his chest. "The first trimester is the riskiest, and I just want to get a little further into it to make sure ..."

He cupped her face in his hands. "It's real. You took that test three times last night with the same results. And it's going to be okay."

She blinked back a tear and nodded.

"Besides," he said, "wouldn't it be nice to know our families were praying for the baby's well-being, too?"

"Yes." She pushed back and waved her hands in the air. "But I have the cutest idea of how to announce it. It's too bad it wasn't around Easter, though. We could have made little egg cards and have them open in the middle like an Easter egg. They could say something like 'hatching this winter ...'"

Sam pulled her into a hug with a chuckle. "You and your cards!"

"It's cute, right?" She laughed with him.

"Just like you." He picked her up and spun her around.

They had been married for six years now. And trying to get pregnant for four. The first year had been exciting, thinking every month would bring the anticipated positive response from the pregnancy test. Instead, they both grew more and more frustrated as nothing happened. They talked with the doctor, who had them chart her temperatures in the mornings and had Faith take Clomid, a common infertility drug. Faith had suffered through mood swings and light-headedness through the five days each month she swallowed those pills, but it had given her hope again. Until six months later, when still nothing had happened.

After that came trips to a fertility specialist. Tears, tests, more fertility drugs, hormone shots, and several different doctors filled the next two years. Sam had stood by her through it all, holding her hand through the appointments, holding her when she cried, holding his head up as they faced the inevitable question from friends and family: "So, when are you going to have kids?"

Faith had quit attending all her friends' baby showers. She would still get them a gift, but she just couldn't force herself to sit through two hours of everyone talking about children and pregnancies and motherhood. Mother's Day had torn her up last year as she watched the youth group hand out roses to all the mamas. Easter also hurt her, and Christmas. She longed to pass on family traditions her parents had started with her for those holidays. Instead, she went through another year of not having a child.

But now ... now she could do all those things. Some of the close friends she had confided in over the last few years had already said they wanted to host her baby shower when it finally happened. She couldn't stop her smile. They were going to be so excited when she shared the news. First, though, she wanted to just enjoy it for herself. She wanted to spend the next few weeks apologizing to God for all the times she had doubted Him and His faithfulness. She wanted to sing like Hannah had done so long ago when she had Samuel. God was good, and He was finally answering her prayers!

"I better get ready for my club meeting." She pulled out of Sam's arms and motioned towards the mess of supplies scattered all over the dining table.

Sam kissed her forehead and left her to it.

Since she sold rubber stamps through a direct sales company, she had been put in charge of the card ministry at church. As she gathered things, she made sure she still had all the slips of paper cut to the right sizes, that all her glue dispensers were full, that she had plenty of scissors, and her ink was still moist. She had come up with an adorable card with an insect stamped in a jar that said, "Heard you caught a bug," on the front. She grinned again as she packed her stamps up in their clear plastic case and rolled her black cart toward the door to put in the car.

"I'm about to go." She called loud enough so Sam could hear her in the back of the house.

He was by her side in an instant. "Let me carry that for you."

She let him take the bag off her shoulder with a smile. "I'm not an invalid, you know. Just pregnant."

"Not *just* pregnant." He gave her a squeeze. "There's no such thing as 'just pregnant.'"

She kissed him before she climbed in the SUV. "I love you."

"I love you, too. Have fun tonight. Be careful."

She pushed the garage door opener and slowly backed her vehicle out of the drive. She and Sam had chosen to live in a quiet suburb instead of closer to town because they liked having a bigger backyard and a house with more character. The church building was in the middle of town so she carefully maneuvered through the evening traffic. She glanced over at her tray of cookies as she had to stop quickly at a light that changed before the driver in front of her had thought it would. She again considered moving the time of their monthly meeting to when there would be less traffic, but many of the women had children and had to work hard to get even this evening off once a month. She couldn't imagine a Saturday morning being easier for them. And most refused to even think about doing something on a Sunday afternoon.

She pulled into the church parking lot and unlocked the door to the fellowship hall. Her best friend, Maysie, pulled in as Faith was bringing in her bags of supplies. She waved as Maysie and her daughter, Kendra, got out and joined her. Kendra was two, and Maysie had a tight hold on the kid-leash Kendra wore on her back. The harness looked like a puppy dog with a very long tail.

"You look like the cat that swallowed the canary." Maysie joined Faith to help lay out the card supplies. Kendra was occupied by a box of chicken nuggets and a package of ketchup. Faith was sure the condiment would be all over the cute top Maysie had dressed the girl in. She made a mental note to always have a bib handy once the baby was here.

"Do I?" Faith was saved from having to say anything else by two other women coming in. She hadn't considered how hard it would be to keep a secret when she was sure the smile on her face was the biggest it had been in a long time.

As three more women filed in, Faith did one last check to make sure she had everything laid out for the three cards she had come up with for this month's get-together. Two had a get-well sentiment, and one had a "thinking of you" theme. She explained the order to put each together as she walked from table to table to make sure everyone was set up.

These nights always flew by as she showed ladies how to use the embossing gun again, refilled the glue widgets, and found an extra pair of scissors here or a few more glue dots there. She made sure one last time that she had all the envelopes addressed for the notes they would send out this week to various sick or mourning or lonely members of their congregation. This ministry was one of the reasons she had joined up with the stamp company to start selling them. It helped her get the products she used for these nights at a lower cost and gave her even more ideas for cards she could make.

They all held hands at the end of the evening for prayer. Kendra's sticky fingers clasped Faith's hand on one side and Maysie's on the other. As they gathered in a circle of friendship, several sick people were mentioned as being in particular need of remembrance.

Maysie, who was going to lead the prayer, looked directly at Faith. "Anything else we need to pray about?"

Faith glanced around at all the others before answering. "Not that I know of."

Maysie asked them all to bow their heads and then thanked God for bringing them together, asked Him to watch over the sick, and then said, "Thank you for our friend, Faith, who loves using her talent to serve you. Thank you for the abilities you have given her and for blessing us all with her in our lives. Please watch over her, whatever she is going through, and give her Your strength and peace. In Jesus' name, Amen."

Faith shot a smile at Maysie before she broke off the circle to give last hugs and finish cleaning up. She pushed in some chairs, gathered up a few more pieces of paper and then packed up the rest of her stamps. She would clean them at home the next day.

"If you want to talk, you have my number." Maysie lifted her tired little girl to her shoulder to carry to the car.

Faith shook her head. Maysie knew a lot of what Faith and Sam had gone through over the last few years. She was one of the dearest and closest friends Faith had besides Sam. Faith made a mental note to make sure that Maysie was at the top of the list of people to tell after family.

She loaded her things into her SUV and headed back onto the roads. Traffic had thinned now that it was past rush hour. The moon hung just over the tops of the buildings as she drove through the quiet town. Her phone buzzed and interrupted her as she was thinking of what she would need to do tomorrow to make sure everything was ready for work next week. Teaching preschool took more prep work than just about any job she could think of.

She slid her finger across the screen. "Hello?"

"Faith, it's your mom." Mom was always very straightforward when she started a phone conversation.

"Hi, Mom. What's up?"

"Are you sitting down, honey?"

Faith rolled her eyes. "I'm driving. Does that count?"

"You girls! Maybe I should just tell you later then." Mom paused. "Why don't you call me when you get home?"

"Is something wrong?"

"Are you almost home?" This didn't come close to answering her question.

"I'll be there in about five minutes." Faith turned into her neighborhood.

"Just call me then." Mom hung up.

That had to be the longest five minutes Faith had ever driven. Had her grandfather had another heart attack? Had Dad lost his job? Maybe her sister was engaged to what's-his-face? Of course, it could just be a cousin expecting a child ... again. Her mom knew how hard it was on her as others in the family seemed to have no problems getting pregnant. She couldn't tell from her mom's tone of voice whether it was a good thing coming or a bad thing.

She pulled into the garage and called Mom as soon as she stepped out of the car. "I'm home now. What's going on?"

"It's Hope."

Faith dropped her keys on the kitchen counter and propped herself on a stool. "What's up with my sister?"

"She lost her job."

Faith wasn't sure why her mom had wanted her sitting down for that news. In this economy, it wasn't really a surprise when people were dismissed. "I'm sorry. Does she have a plan?"

"Well, that's what I'm calling you about." Mom's voice hinted of something Faith wasn't going to like.

Faith cocked an eyebrow, even though her mom couldn't see it. "Oh?"

"I was thinking maybe she could stay with you this summer and work with you at that summer camp. Then, maybe she could find a job there in the fall. They say there's more teaching jobs available in Texas than any other state right now."

"Mom, they just had a bunch of layoffs. I'm not sure she'd have any more luck here than in Mississippi." Faith shook her head. "I'm also not sure I'll be working as a counselor this summer. I haven't decided yet." In all honesty, she wasn't sure her doctor would like the thought of her out in the Texas heat all day long, wrangling kids at a summer camp, with her being about three months pregnant by then. But she wasn't going to tell her mom that tonight ... not after the discussion she had had with Sam earlier.

He walked into the kitchen and gave her a look to ask whom she was talking to. She mouthed the word "mom" and he gave a nod.

"But she could still work there, right?" Mom asked.

"Are you sure she'd even want to? She hates Texas." Faith picked at a spot she had missed with the dishrag on the counter.

"I'm talking her into it. I think it would be good for her to try something new."

"Let me talk to Sam about it, and we'll see. I'm not making any promises. But we'll see." Faith gave Sam a "tell you later" wave as he turned to face her.

Mom sighed. "Okay. But let me know soon. I'm trying to help her figure all this out so she can know what to do about her apartment lease that would have to be renewed at the end of June."

"Okay, Mom. Promise." Faith shook her head. "Give her my love, and I'll get back to you about the rest."

She hung up and looked at her husband. "Hope lost her job. Mom thinks she could find a job easier down here and that maybe she should live with us for a few months."

Sam put both hands on the counter, looked right in Faith's eyes, and said, "No."

CHAPTER 3

HOPE

When Kyle called soon after Hope's conversation with her mom, Hope was quick to agree to go out to dinner with him that evening. At the Mexican restaurant, Hope let herself relax for the first time since that morning. The tantalizing aromas of onions, peppers, and tomatoes mingled irresistibly with the scent of grilling tortillas. Her stomach rumbled in appreciation. She dipped a chip in salsa and munched on it while Kyle mulled over what he wanted. She always got the same thing: the enchiladas.

"I can never decide what sounds good here. What should I get?" He flicked the edge of his menu over and over.

She took a drink of water to wash down her chip. "You know what I get. What are you in the mood for?"

"Italian."

"Well, then we're in the wrong place. You like the quesadillas."

He glanced at her over the plastic folder in his hands before returning his gaze to the options. "I guess."

"Or the nachos are good."

"Yeah ..." There was no conviction in his voice.

The waiter came and asked if they were ready. Hope looked at Kyle, and he just shrugged. She placed her order and then waited while Kyle hemmed and hawed a few more moments before deciding on the nachos.

She dipped another chip in the salsa and closed her eyes as the bite of peppers hit her tongue. She could eat Mexican food every day of the week and not get tired of it. She opened her eyes when Kyle took her hand.

"Long day?" He absent-mindedly ran his thumb over her skin.

Was he kidding right now? He knew what all had happened today. Did he think any of it was a good thing?

"Well …" She couldn't keep all the sarcasm from her voice. "I lost both my job and my car this afternoon. And my mom wants me to move away from here. So, yeah, I'd say it's been a long day."

"You don't have to be so snarky about it." He leaned back in his chair and let go of his grip on her. "Tell me again how you hit a school bus."

"The roads were wet." She waved her hand in the air. "My brakes decided they'd done their duty and to not work as I got to the intersection of Mays and Breaker. I slid through before the school bus cleared it all the way, and we collided."

"I'm surprised your air bags didn't deploy."

"I wasn't going that fast to begin with, and the brakes worked just well enough to slow me down more. But it made the hood of my car look like an accordion." She dipped another chip with more force than necessary, cringing as a chunk broke off in the dish.

"And your job? What happened there? I thought your principal loved you." Kyle crossed his arms.

Hope sighed. "He did love me. Just not enough to negate the fact that I was the last one hired so I'm the first one to be cut. They need another football coach for next year and since one of the few things coaches teach is math, they decided it would be easier to find than a coach that teaches English, which is the other position they need to fill. It could change by August, but with all the cutbacks in education right now, they're almost one hundred percent sure they're not going to be able to hire me back."

Kyle sprinkled some extra salt on his chip before stuffing it in his mouth. She wondered again how high his sodium levels must be, the way he abused that shaker all the time, but she didn't say anything tonight.

"I'm going to start reaching out to some of the other schools in the area. Oxford is big enough. There shouldn't be a problem for me to find another job. I mean, everyone needs math teachers." Hope nodded her head as if to assure herself.

"So why does your mom think you should move?"

"For some reason, she's got it in her head that it's going to be easier for me to find a position in Texas, where Faith lives. I don't know why she thinks Texas is the only state hiring teachers. But she wants me to go live with Faith and Sam this summer and do that summer camp Faith has done the last couple of years so I can have some extra money stashed back 'just in case.'" Hope used her fingers to form air quotes.

"And Faith is okay with that?"

Hope shrugged. "Like my mom asked first?"

"Well …" The noisiness of his chewing amped her nerves up even higher. "I'm sorry your day was so bad. Good thing Cassidy was off work and could pick you up."

"Yeah." Hope played with the wrapper that held her knife and fork together. "Where were you? I tried calling you first."

"Oh. Study session ran long. We've got a group project due at the end of the week, and Susan thought it needed some extra tweaking, so we had to spend a couple hours in the library this afternoon. I had my phone on vibrate and didn't feel it go off."

"What class is that for?" Hope asked.

"World History. Just a few more history credits and I can actually have a minor in it when I graduate."

"In May?" Hope glanced up at him.

"No way. Since I switched to political science as my major last fall, I've got at least another three semesters ahead of me. Maybe more." Kyle shrugged.

"I've been meaning to ask you, what exactly will you do with a political science degree?" Hope broke a chip in two.

"I could go into politics. Or teaching. Or something like that. Maybe I'll go on one of those radio shows and just talk about politics."

"Huh." Did her voice fully convey to him the skepticism running through her at that moment?

"It's going to be great. I know it took me a while to find out what I was interested in, but now, I'm in it for the long run. No more changes in major. That should make my parents happy." Kyle laughed.

Hope studied him across the tile-topped table. His brown hair was wavy and curled over his ears a bit. He tossed his head to the side to get the long pieces out of his brown eyes. She had thought he was cute when they first met, but now he just struck her as being rather sloppy.

"Your hair's getting long." She pointed to his head.

"Isn't that the style?" He gave a cocky grin. "I can get some of those skinny jeans and high-top tennis shoes, and I'll be emo all over."

"I think that style looks ridiculous. That's the way a bunch of the boys in my class dress." Hope shook her head.

"So, you're saying I'm trying to look like a teenager?"

"Well, you are going to be twenty-six later this year." She cut her eyes up at him.

"And that makes me old?"

"Not old. Just old enough to know better than to dress like a teenager." She lifted a shoulder as if that should be obvious.

"Right." He sounded a bit wounded.

"I'm just thinking if you're going to go into politics, maybe you should start looking the part now." She had no idea why she had brought this up in the first place. What was it about him tonight that was making him so annoying? Usually, they got along fine. Didn't they? "That will make it easier to get a job and stuff after school so we can finally get married."

He jerked his head up from the chip he was salting. "Whoa! Who said anything about marriage?"

She gave him an incredulous look. "Isn't that why people date? So they can get married eventually? I mean, I'm not in any hurry or anything ..."

"I have absolutely no desire to get married."

Their food arrived before Hope could reply. She held her hands back as the hot plate was placed in front of her. The steam coming off of her enchiladas was nothing compared to the heat coming out her ears. Kyle dug right into his nachos like everything in the world was perfect.

She ate a bite of her dinner while she figured out how to continue their discussion. The cheese stretched what had to be at least twelve inches before breaking as she lifted a second bite to her mouth and enjoyed the flavors of meat and sauce. Kyle didn't look like he even remembered what they had been talking about.

"Where do you see us in five years?" She pushed around her rice and refried beans.

"Five years? That's like an eternity from now. I don't know where I'll be in five years." Kyle flicked an olive off the bite on his fork and then stuffed the rest in his mouth.

She noticed he said, "I," instead of, "we." "Okay, two years then. Where do you see us in two years?"

"Well, like I said, I might graduate in a year and a half. I guess I'll probably try to find a job after that. Or maybe travel for a while. I don't know. I usually don't even know what I'm doing the next day, Hope. Why does it matter so much?"

"Why does it matter so much?" She threw her napkin down on the table. "It matters so much because I'm the kind of person who knew exactly what she wanted to be when she grew up—from the age of three! I laid out a plan, and now I've got my bachelor's and master's in education. You, on the other hand, started college seven years ago — seven years! You started as an art major, then, after a year, decided you'd rather do biology and become a doctor. That lasted a year and a half. After that, you wanted to be an engineer, right?"

"What does this have to do with anything?" He broke a chip into tiny pieces.

"It has to do with the fact that evidently this relationship is going exactly where your life is going."

He threw his napkin down, too. "And where exactly might that be?"

"Nowhere." Hope waved the server over to get a to-go box.

∼

"You should go." Cassidy sat beside Hope on their sofa eating ice cream later that evening.

Hope looked up around a spoonful of rocky road. "Go?"

"To Texas. For the summer."

Hope wrinkled her nose. "I hate Texas."

"Have you ever been to Texas?" Cassidy pointed her spoon at Hope.

"No, but that doesn't mean I'll like it when I get there."

Cassidy folded her long legs underneath her and stared at Hope. "Hope, it would be good for you to get away and figure out what happened between you and Kyle. Just because you think it's completely over and unfixable, that doesn't mean it is. He still likes you. And you must have seen something in him, or you wouldn't have started dating in the first place."

"He's a professional student who never wants to get married. Nothing *can* happen between the two of us." Hope shook her head.

"But he might change his mind."

"Like he changes his major?" Hope raised an eyebrow.

"You know what they always say: 'Absence makes the heart grow fonder.'" Cassidy used a sing-song voice.

"What if I don't want to work things out with Kyle? What if I just want to find another teaching job here, where I know the people around me are going to root for the right football team? Not in some redneck state that thinks boots are black-tie wear." Hope moaned.

"Having never been to Texas, you don't know what they wear. Your sister doesn't wear boots all the time."

"But she does own a pair."

"I had no idea you were so stuck up." Cassidy turned to fully face her.

"What? I'm not stuck up."

"You're unwilling to go hang out with your sister and earn a little extra money just because she lives in another state, one you haven't even been to. You realize, don't you, that most people feel just as adversely towards Mississippi as you do towards evidently all forty-nine other states? Come on, Miss Stubborn. What could it really hurt to live in a state where people wear boots? They wear boots in Tennessee, too, ya know, and you used to live there."

"But those are more like fancy boots for singing country music in." Hope threw out the only argument she could think of, lame as it was. She was still reeling from being called "stuck up."

"You own a pair of roller skates, but that doesn't mean you're going out for roller derby." Cassidy paused and cocked her head. "Although that would be so cool."

Hope frowned.

"Okay, so that point didn't work as well out loud as it did in my head, but Hope, for real. Think about it. You were frustrated with your job anyway. You said the kids hated geometry and you wanted to give them all the grades they deserved instead of continuing to dumb down your curriculum. You were tired of fighting with the coaches about how to get their players' grades up high enough to play. You love teaching, but maybe you need a break and this is God's way of giving you one." Cassidy leaned back and folded her arms.

"Since when did God start telling you His plans for me?" Hope asked.

"He didn't. I'm just saying maybe you should at least consider what your mom is suggesting. She's a pretty smart lady, you know."

Hope threw a pillow at her roommate. "You just like her because she always sends your favorite cookies when she sends me some, too."

"That's how I know she's smart." Cassidy laughed.

"But what about you? That will leave you in the lurch for rent for a couple months."

"Actually, I may have that worked out." Cassidy gave her a sheepish look.

"Oh?"

"My cousin Amy was looking for somewhere to intern this summer and may have found a position here. I was trying to figure out how I was going to squeeze her in with the two of us and all our stuff packed in here so tightly already and then this happened." Cassidy threw her hands up in the air. "Like I said, maybe God's trying to tell you something."

"So, you're kicking me out?" Hope knew her voice sounded whiny, but she didn't care.

"No, silly. I want you to come back in the fall. I'm just saying I'll be okay if you decide to go."

Hope leaned back against the armrest. "If God is trying to tell me something, I wish He had picked a gentler way."

CHAPTER 4

FAITH

"You're not even willing to consider it at all?" Faith glanced at Sam as she cut up carrots for the salad. It was a week after she had first pitched her mom's proposal to him of Hope moving in with them for the summer. He hadn't budged an inch on his original answer.

"Whenever you two get together, she makes you mad. You never get along. You don't need that stress right now." Sam picked up the platter of steaks to take them out to the grill. "There's nothing to consider."

Faith finished making the salad and checked on the baking potatoes. She thought back over the last six years of marriage to Sam. He had never been unreasonable. She agreed that she and Hope didn't always see eye to eye, but wasn't that what sisters did? Weren't they supposed to squabble?

Everyone always said that siblings grew closer as they grew older. Growing up, she had time and again been counseled that there would come a season in her life when she would love her sister and wish they could spend more time together. And over the last few years, there had been a few moments of peace between them during family get-togethers.

Of course, then Hope would spout off something she thought she knew more about than Faith or point out what Faith was doing wrong. Or she would criticize Sam's teaching style. Or she would scoff at their home state. Sam was right. They did seem to fight a lot when they got together.

She pulled glasses down and put ice in them, glancing through the window at her husband. She still had to find a way to convince him that they needed to do this. Something had tugged at her heartstrings when Mom suggested Hope move in with them for the summer. Faith would be less guilt-ridden about not working at Camp TwinCreeks this summer if she could offer her sister as a replacement, although she was going to miss it like crazy. And who knew? Maybe they could work through some of their differences if they were forced to be together every day.

Sam walked back in, smelling of charcoal smoke and sweat. She breathed in deeply as she hugged him. He kissed the top of her head and sighed.

"Why are you so bound and determined to add this stress to your life?" He ran his fingers down the side of her cheeks. "Stress isn't good for the baby."

She leaned back against the island and studied him. What could she say to change his mind? Why *was* she so desperate to do this? Why was this so important to her?

An idea struck her. "What if it were Charlie?"

"What?"

"What if it were Charlie?" She crossed her arms. "What if it were your brother instead of my sister needing a place to stay? A way to make some extra money this summer?"

"But it's not." Sam propped himself against the counter opposite her.

She poked him in the chest. "But what if it were. Would you agree to it then?"

"That's completely different, and you know it. Charlie ... Charlie isn't like your sister. He has anxiety issues and can't face new situations easily."

"So you're saying if he needed a place to stay, you'd be okay with it because he has social anxiety?"

"No, Faith. Stop putting words in my mouth. I'm just saying that you can't compare this situation to one with Charlie because there are too many differing factors. Hope and Charlie are nothing alike."

"What about Andy? Would you be okay with Andy living with us for the summer?" Faith put her hands on her hips.

"Andy is fifteen."

"And?"

Sam gave her a look of exasperation. "And so that situation is completely different too."

"Let's just say for the sake of argument that Andy is twenty and needs a job for the summer. He can't find one where your parents are, so he looks at coming down here and working at camp just to make money so he can pay for his textbooks. Would you be okay with that, Samuel Landon McCreary?"

"What is this? A courtroom?" Sam went back outside to check the steaks.

Faith threw the dishcloth down in the sink to let out some frustration. Sam didn't always get along with his brothers, just like she didn't always get along with her sister. She knew part of that was because there were five years between each sibling in his family, but she still thought she had a valid point. He was treating her sister differently than he would one of his brothers.

She went and flopped down in a chair in the living room. The fan felt good on her hot face as it stirred the air a bit more than in the kitchen. Texas summer heat was already kicking in even though May wouldn't start until tomorrow. She knew there was no way she would be able to work at camp this summer and be out in the hundred-degree temperatures every day the way she had the last couple of summers. In some ways, she was sad about that as she had loved working with the kids. But in truth, she would give up just about anything to be in the situation she was in now, pregnant with her first child.

Sam stood by her chair and stroked her hair. "I'm sorry."

"I'm sorry, too." She looked up at him. "I guess I just feel like you're handling this situation unfairly. I know she and I haven't always gotten along, but this is our house and if she starts causing problems, we can let her know that she doesn't have to stay here anymore."

"I just want to have that relationship with my sister that everyone always told me I'd have when we grew up ... the kind where we liked each other." Faith laughed. "Maybe God's giving us a chance to work on that and see if we can start seeing more eye to eye."

"And what if you still don't get that relationship?" Sam knelt down to look her in the eyes.

"Then I'll just have to keep working toward it." Faith touched his head. "She's my sister in Christ as well as my sister in the flesh. That means I should work even harder to get along with her, right?"

He kissed her forehead and then stood up. "Come eat. We'll pray about it some more, but you'll probably get your way just like you always do."

"I take offense at that." She pushed him from behind. "You got to choose where we put the Christmas tree last year!"

∼

TWO WEEKS LATER, Faith answered the phone, knowing what her mom was going to say. They had sent the Mother's Day cards with the news of the coming baby.

"Faith Sarah, why didn't you tell me?" Mom asked over the line.

"Because I wanted it to be a surprise for Mother's Day." Faith laughed.

"When are you due?"

"Late December. Maybe we'll have a Christmas baby." Faith put her hand over her stomach even though it was still early to be showing.

Mom chuckled. "Poor child. Are we rooting for a boy or a girl?"

"We're just glad to be able to finally have a child. I don't care as long as it's healthy."

"I completely understand, Darling. That's the way your father and I felt when we finally had you."

"I thought you said I came just like you planned."

"I didn't bring this up earlier because I didn't want you to feel like I was butting in and trying to make your experience out to be exactly like mine." Mom sighed. "Remember when you first started seeing that things weren't working like you had planned? And I mentioned that your father and I had gone through several rounds of fertility drugs, too, so not to be too scared of them?"

Faith frowned. "Yeah, but you sounded like it worked pretty quickly after that. And you've always led me to believe that you didn't have to do anything else."

"Well, we actually miscarried a couple of times before we were blessed with you. It took us over four years to finally have you and then two more to have your sister. They didn't have quite as much in the ways of fertility treatments back then, but they had hormones similar to what you've been on. Every time I thought I was finally going to have a child, I felt like God took it away again. That's why we named you the way we did."

"Faith Sarah?" Faith and Hope had always joked that they were named after the verse in I Corinthians. It was a great thing, they'd say, they didn't have another sister because she would have been named Charity, and then she would have been "the greatest of these." She hadn't realized there was a real reason she was named Faith.

"*Faith* because that's what I developed more than anything during those years. I thought I had a solid faith in God from the day I was baptized—until the day we started trying to get pregnant. I realized quickly, though, that it had never been tested. I had a lot of rough nights where I was angry at God, thought He hated me and didn't care." Mom's voice was quiet, full of emotion even after all these years.

"Mom, why didn't you tell me this? That's exactly the way I felt going through what we've gone through over the last four years." Faith sobbed. "I thought I was all alone in this."

"No, Sweetie. You were never alone. You always had God. And Sam. And I was here praying for you the whole time. I just didn't want you to feel like I was always comparing my situation to yours or that yours was worse or easier or anything. I was here to listen and support."

"But it would have been nice to know I had your empathy, too, Mom. I felt like I was the only one in our family who had to go through all this stupid fertility stuff. And in the end, we weren't even trying when it finally worked!"

"I'm sorry, Faith. I guess I just figured it would keep you from developing your own faith if I shared more of my experience. That's something only God can help you with."

Faith wiped the tears from her cheeks.

"I'm really glad it finally worked, Honey." Mom's voice was soft.

"I know, Mom. Thanks."

"I love you."

"I love you, too."

"Have you thought any more about your sister coming?" Mom's abrupt subject change left Faith's head spinning.

She choked out a laugh. "Oh, Mom. Maybe. I'm still working on Sam, but he's coming around."

"Good."

"Are you sure this is going to work out as well as you think it will?" Faith propped her feet up on the coffee table.

"Of course I am." Mom's voice sounded offended. "Why wouldn't it?"

CHAPTER 5

HOPE

Hope glared at her GPS app as it told her once again it was recalculating. She hated having to use it, but her Dad had insisted it would be the best means for her to find her way to Faith's house. Once she passed Texarkana, the land was flat and boring. She sighed as she passed another field of cattle.

Her dad had come down to Oxford the week after her wreck and helped her find a new car. He insisted on checking everything out and then financing it for her. She had objected, but he hushed her.

"This way, you can pay me back when you can, and you'll get a lower interest rate." He had pressed the keys into her hand.

"It's too much."

"You're my baby. It's what a dad does for his baby."

She ran her hands over the smooth dash of the new-to-her Ford and smiled in spite of herself. Sometimes, it was nice to let her dad take care of her. The GPS finally figured out where she was going and displayed that she had an estimated three more hours. She was just through Dallas, headed south toward Austin.

She had dropped off most of her possessions at her parents' house the week before. Her mother had taken her shopping for more camp-friendly clothes and extra sunscreen. She had fattened up on all her favorite meals, and then her mom and dad had loaded her new car and sent her west.

It had been hard to leave Buckley, a job she had once considered her dream. A few kids had asked, "But Ms. C, who will teach us algebra next year?" There was still no promise of employment the next fall, but she couldn't focus on that yet. She was headed to her sister's house for a summer job.

Faith had set up a phone interview with the camp director around mid-May, and he said she sounded perfect. She would go to some training sessions the next Monday and then straight into work right after Memorial Day. Since she already had her CPR training, she got to come down later than some of the other counselors. She still wasn't sure what age group she would end up with, but she had requested girls. This was definitely going to be different than teaching high school math.

She hadn't talked to Faith since this all started, though. Every plan and action had gone through Mom. Come to think of it, she was pretty sure she hadn't spoken to her sister since the Christmas before.

It wasn't always like that. They were brought up in the same bedroom for the first eight years of Hope's life. Faith had been Hope's ride from the day Faith got her license until she went to college. They had been in the same youth group and gone to the same school. Hope wasn't really sure what it was about her older sister that drove her so crazy.

Even though they were only a few years apart in age, Hope had been more of a social butterfly while Faith was more of a brainiac and lover of the visual arts. They had both gone through piano lessons and been in chorus, but Hope had stuck with it longer while Faith dropped out to dabble in painting classes and National Honor Society. It wasn't really that one was more intelligent than the other. They were just ... different. Faith had her arts and crafts, and Hope had her music and math.

Hope had many boyfriends through the years, while Faith hadn't dated anyone until she met Sam in college. Her brother-in-law was okay, but her sister could have done better than a basketball coach for a Christian high school. Didn't he know public school teachers made much more than the ones at private schools?

Mom had shared Faith's news about the coming baby. This was one good thing about having a brother-in-law. Hope would finally get to be an aunt. She couldn't wait to spoil her baby niece or nephew. She smiled as she drove through the south side of Waco. Just over an hour to go.

She put in a CD from when she was in chorus in college and sang along as praises to God filled the car. She was trying to be more like her Heavenly Father, reading the Bible each morning and making a point to keep a prayer journal in the evening. It had helped her through the last month and a half, she could tell, although she still wasn't sure what God had planned for her. She just hoped all the readings and prayers would help her through whatever lay ahead this summer.

The GPS at last directed her through an older neighborhood outside one of the northern suburbs of Austin. She studied the homes and yards. It wasn't modern, but it had personality. Brick covered the front of the ranch-style structure, with a tree shading most of the front yard. The garage and front door were painted a dark green. Curtains were pulled back from the windows to let in natural light. It suited Faith perfectly.

She pulled into the driveway and parked next to Sam's pick-up truck. Faith ran out the door and hugged Hope as soon as she had gotten out of her car.

Where did that come from? Hope couldn't remember the last time Faith had greeted her like this. Definitely not since they became teenagers. She hesitated, then gave a tentative return squeeze.

Faith leaned back and grinned. "I'm glad you made it safely. Now maybe Mom will quit calling to see if you're here yet."

"So that's the only reason you're glad I'm safe?" Hope bumped her door closed.

"No, but it does take away the promise of another call from Mom this evening. You can go phone her and let her know you're here. Then, I'll show you around, and we can catch up." Faith took a bag out of Hope's hands.

"That's pretty heavy, Faith. Why don't you carry this one instead?" Hope held out a small make-up case.

"Hope, I'm pregnant. As long as it's not over twenty-five pounds, I'm okay."

"I don't know. I think Dad might tell you that one is over twenty-five pounds." Hope gave a grin of her own.

The girls walked into the house and the aroma of garlic and tomatoes arrested Hope's senses, causing her stomach to rumble in response. Sam stood at the stove and waved his spatula at her as they walked by to go down a carpeted hallway. Faith opened a door to a room with a huge picture window looking out to the backyard. A twin bed stood in the corner away from it, and a rocking chair sat next to the window. Faith's old dresser from when she was a teenager stood next to the bed.

"It's not much. And it may change a bit even while you're here. This is going to be the nursery." Faith set the bag down on the dresser. "But I figure it will work for you this summer, too. Not like we have any baby furniture or anything yet. Maybe I can get you to help me paint it while you're here, though."

"I can probably do that." Hope set her other bag and suitcase next to the bed. "Where did you get this picture?"

Faith leaned over to look at the print of the two of them as small girls sitting in a field of flowers. She smiled. "I stole it from Mom and blew it up. Thought it would be perfect for a little girl's room."

"You're having a girl?" Hope asked.

"Not sure yet. But it's fun to tease Sam about." Faith laughed. "Anyway, I emptied the dresser so it's free for you to use. And there's closet space. The curtains draw closed if you just unhook them at the sides so you can have some privacy in the evenings."

"It's great, Faith. Really."

"There's towels in the cabinets above the toilet in the bathroom and washcloths in the drawer by the sink."

Hope followed her sister back down the hall to see the bathroom.

Faith opened cabinet doors to show the contents. "If you need anything, just let us know. Now that we've lived here a couple years, I think even Sam knows where everything is."

"Hey!" His voice carried down the hall from the kitchen. "I heard that."

Hope returned to the room that would be hers this summer. Hers and her future niece's, she corrected herself. She tried to picture it with a crib and a changing table. She sat on the edge of the bed that matched the one she had slept on growing up.

Faith's welcome had definitely been warmer than expected. If Hope were honest with herself, she hadn't been sure how her sister would act. With their mother as good as forcing them into this situation, it wasn't like they were starting off on the best foot to begin with. With their recent history of disagreements, that made things even more volatile. But if Faith could act like everything was perfect, so could Hope. Maybe Faith's hormones were making her nicer? Hope shook her head. That wasn't kind. Best to take things at face value until proven otherwise, right?

Everything seemed to be great. She was here safe and sound—she'd call Mom in a minute to let her know. The house was nice and cool compared to the heat outside. Faith and Sam had been friendly. She had a job starting Monday that would give her a cushion of money just in case ... well, she wouldn't finish that scenario in her head. She *would* find a job for the fall, but it would still be nice to have the extra funds. So, with everything going so right, why did she feel like everything was falling apart even more now that she was here?

CHAPTER 6

FAITH

Faith turned in the front seat of her SUV to look back at Hope. "I'm going to introduce you to Maria and Joe Hernandez today. She works in the office at camp, and he is a counselor. They're the ones who got me started working there several years ago."

Hope just nodded.

Faith faced the front again and Sam squeezed her hand as they wove through the neighborhood and into town. Faith loved Sunday mornings. Everything seemed more at peace, slower. Sam parked by the classroom wing of the church building and they all piled out. Hope followed as Sam and Faith led the way down the hall.

"We usually go to this class. We're studying John the Baptist right now. But there's other classes if you want to see what's available." Faith stopped at the doorway.

"Afraid I might say something to embarrass you?" Hope cocked an eyebrow.

"No. I just didn't want you to feel like you had to go to this class just because we do. It's up to you." Faith refused to give in to her sister's jibes.

"This is fine." Hope walked in to sit down near Sam.

Faith couldn't help but wonder what all her sister was thinking. They hadn't talked much the night before as Hope had claimed exhaustion and headed to bed soon after dinner. This morning she had gotten up in time for breakfast but still hadn't said much. All through class, Faith stole glances at her sister, but Hope for the most part kept her eyes on her Bible and ignored everything going on around her.

Was Faith trying too hard? Had she overwhelmed Hope when she ran out and hugged and gushed yesterday? She didn't think she had been over-exuberant, but she also hadn't spent any real time with her sister over the last few years except a day or two at holidays. She didn't know her sister anymore. Getting hugged by a stranger would be a bit awkward. Could you be a stranger to someone you grew up with?

Faith tried to draw her attention back to what the teacher was saying about John, but her mind bounced back and forth between the Bible study and her sister. Was this a bad idea after all? Had Sam been right? It had been less than twenty-four hours and already they weren't talking. *You're overreacting and overthinking. Stop it, Faith Sarah!* She gave herself a mental shake and tried to focus once again on what she was supposed to be doing.

Worship was much the same way, although Hope did participate. Her soprano voice had always blended well with Faith's alto. Several people close by turned to smile at the sisters as they praised God side by side. Their voices did what they themselves couldn't do—got along in perfect harmony.

Faith introduced Hope to Maria after services. Maria was petite but fiery and fun-loving. The Hernandezes had been some of the first in the congregation to welcome Sam and Faith when they moved to the area, and the two families had been close ever since. Faith looked around for Maria's son but didn't see him.

"If you're looking for Joe, he's not here. He had to help move a friend this weekend and is supposed to be driving back this afternoon," Maria said with her slightly Latina accent.

"Bummer. I was going to introduce him to Hope so she would know someone there tomorrow." Faith shrugged.

"Joe is always good to go help friends whenever they ask, even if it means last-minute and not at a convenient time to him. He didn't know he was going until Friday and then left first thing yesterday morning to help drive the truck. Crazy boy." Maria's voice was full of love for her son.

"Joe sort of grew up at Camp TwinCreeks." Faith turned to Hope. "He started as a camper and has worked as a counselor since he was a teenager. Maria helped start it almost thirty years ago."

"Neat." Hope nodded.

"I hope you love it there, too, Hope." Maria reached out and squeezed her arm. "It's really a fun place to work."

"I'm sure it will be great." Hope gave a slight smile. It didn't reach all the way to her eyes. "I'm going on out to the car if that's okay with you."

"Sure." Faith handed her a set of keys.

"She looks lost." Maria stood with Faith and watched Hope walk away.

"I don't know how to reach her. We haven't really been close since we were little. So much has gone wrong in her life lately that I wonder what all she's thinking and feeling, but she's hardly talked to me since she got here. Just a few words to get through dinner last night and breakfast this morning. It's almost like she's set herself up to hate everything about this summer and she's only doing it for Mom."

"Maybe she just needs to get adjusted. It's hard to leave your home and go somewhere else. My family did that when we moved here from Mexico when I was a little girl. Give her time." Maria hugged Faith to her side and held on for a moment.

Faith nodded and then waved to Sam that they should go.

He caught up with her as she walked down the hallway. "Where's Hope?"

"She went on out to the car. She rather reminds me of a zombie today. I'm not sure how to get her to open up." Faith sighed. "I don't want her to be miserable, but I can't help if she won't tell me what's wrong."

"I know you're a fixer, Faith, but sometimes people just need to work things through by themselves. Give her time."

"That's what Maria suggested, too."

"So, it must be right." He playfully bumped hips with her.

"Wait a minute. Isn't 'fixer' what you call my mom?" She poked him in the side as they exited the building. "And not in a nice way?"

He raised his eyebrows. "I love your mom."

"That's not what I asked."

"Sweetheart, you have one of the biggest hearts in Texas, and that means you want everyone to be happy and have everything perfect. Unfortunately, sometimes you seem to think you can make that happen. You try to fix things." He raised a shoulder. "It's not always a bad thing, but sometimes things can't be fixed. Sometimes, there's just bad in this world because of its fallen state. You and your mom don't always agree with that."

Faith didn't say anything. The way he explained it made it sound less bad, but also like something she might need to work on … or was that the "fixer" in her trying to make things perfect? She climbed into the car, grateful that Hope had already turned it on so the air conditioner could start cooling things off. If she was already this hot and miserable at the end of May, how was she ever going to make it all summer with this pregnancy?

Hope was quiet all the way home and disappeared to her room right after lunch. Faith left her alone. She would take Maria's and Sam's advice for now, but she would also keep an eye on her sister.

∼

Hope

Hope stared at herself in the bathroom mirror. She wasn't ready.

Why had she agreed to do this? Camp wasn't her thing. Sweating and running around with little kids and miles from home. She ran a hand over her stomach to calm the butterflies, then grabbed her toothbrush. Too late now.

"You've got your water bottle?" Faith asked as she walked by the open door.

"Yes." Hope's reply was a bit muffled as she tried not to choke on the toothpaste.

"Sunscreen?"

Hope rolled her eyes. "Yes, *Mom*."

Faith stuck her head in the bathroom. "I've just done this before and am trying to help you out. Sorry if I'm coming across as too motherly for you."

"I know. But I have everything. And if I don't, you're only a text away." Hope dried her mouth on the towel.

"What about —" Faith stopped when Hope gave her a dirty look.

"You took me out there yesterday and showed me around. I know how to get there and back. They're supplying lunch. I've got all the forms I'm supposed to turn in today along with my ID. I've got sunscreen, extra water, and my swimsuit, just in case. I'm wearing tennis shoes like you said to. I've got sunglasses and a writing utensil. I'll be fine. Besides, you're coming by at lunch to see if they really do need you for a couple of weeks while the crafts counselor goes on vacation. I'll be fine."

Faith held her hands up in surrender. "You're right. I'm sorry."

Hope shrugged. "Just practicing for when my niece gets here, right?"

"Have fun today. I love you." Faith wrapped Hope in a hug before Hope could escape.

"Love you, too." Hope's reply was automatic.

The cool morning was misleading, but Hope wouldn't complain about it only being 75. Faith had told her it would be hot by lunchtime and to enjoy the early hours.

Hope drove several miles outside of town to the camp she would be working at for the next two months. On a day when most people would be barbecuing and hanging out with family, she was going to learn the ropes of her new summer job. She found a parking place between two trucks and walked up to the main building.

Only the offices and craft room had air conditioning. Everything else was open, so breezes could pass through. And it helped that there were still quite a few trees around, although they looked more like really tall shrubs compared to the towering pines and oaks of Mississippi. At least they provided some shade.

The campus was several acres with a centralized building for the offices, nurse's station, snack area, and main gathering place. A small trailer served as the arts and crafts room. Several other structures were around, but they didn't have walls. They just provided a bit of protection for the groups who gathered under them. A soccer field was near the front fence, with the pool, playground, and miniature golf area between it and the main building. Towards the back of the property was a petting area that housed some goats, pigs, rabbits, and chickens, as well as a separate stable area for horseback riding. There was also an archery range, a BB gun range, and a climbing tower with zipline for the older kids. Hope had to admit that the set-up was rather impressive. As a child, she probably would have enjoyed a week or two here in the summers.

She signed in just inside the door and got her name tag. After she turned in her forms and let them copy her driver's license, she scanned the area to see where to sit. Other people were milling about the large room, some greeting each other with great enthusiasm and others who looked more like they didn't know anyone else there, either. She was about to just pick whatever seat she could find farthest from anyone else when someone caught her arm.

She turned to face a Latino man just taller than herself. He gave a wide smile and stuck out his hand to shake. "I'm Joe."

"Maria's Joe?" Hope asked as she realized the connection between the woman she had met the day before and this guy. She had been expecting a teenager or someone just out of high school, not someone around her own age and well-built and handsome. He was tanned with dark hair cut short and slightly spiky. His eyes were chocolate brown and crinkled at the corners like he smiled all the time.

"She's my mom, yeah." He nodded. "I'm also the associate minister at church. And I pick up odd jobs here and there. Like being a counselor here. Faith has done nothing but talk about you coming for the last few weeks. You all settled in and ready for a fun summer?"

Hope found it hard to believe her sister could have been quite as excited as Joe made it sound. She shrugged in reply to his question. "I guess."

"Oh, come on. Free sun tan. Playing every day. Horses. Swimming. Archery." Joe motioned around them as if showing off the prizes of a game show. "This is the best place in the world to spend summer."

"Somehow I really don't think my skin is going to tan as well as yours." Hope held up a very white arm. "Maybe I'll get so many freckles that they'll all run together and look like a tan."

"Whatever works for you." He gave a huge grin, and Hope couldn't help but smile in return.

During the beginning of the morning, they all got to learn the history of TwinCreeks, how a sweet couple had decided that this piece of land would be perfect for a summer camp and had added buildings and sheds and horses over the last twenty-five years. They each stood up and told a little bit about themselves at the direction of the head counselor, Steve. "We're going to be a team helping these kids have the best summer they can have. But we can only do that by working together."

Joe volunteered to be first. He seemed to be the most exuberant person there, even more than the director. "I'm Joe. I have been at Camp TwinCreeks for the last twenty-one years. I started as a mini camper, and now I'm the only one they trust first-grade boys with."

"That's because you still think like a first-grade boy." Hope couldn't see who had called out the tease, but she laughed along with everyone else.

Hope regretted sitting next to Joe when she realized she was next. "I'm Hope. I'm actually just visiting Texas for the summer to earn a little money before school starts back. Normally, I teach high school math in Oxford, Mississippi. Go Rebels!" She probably shouldn't have thrown that last bit in, considering the dirty looks that shot around the room, but she couldn't help herself.

The others one-by-one did their own little spiels, telling how many years they had been there or if they were students somewhere or not. Most of the counselors were college students. College seemed a lifetime ago, even though Hope had only been out herself for a couple of years. Would she have anything in common with these people?

The rest of the morning focused on team-building exercises. They broke into different groups, going from activity to activity. A scavenger hunt had clues hidden over the whole campus to help people get accustomed to where things were. Water relays had her and her teammates passing leaking balloons over their heads to the one behind to see who could fill their bucket the highest. And the knot activity meant everyone grabbed two other hands in the middle and then worked together to untangle themselves. She would never admit to anyone that she was glad to have been put in Joe's group ... or that she had purposely grabbed his hand in the last event. There was much laughter and chaos as the morning passed into the heat of the afternoon.

Hope wiped her forehead with the back of her hand and took a swig from her water bottle as Faith walked up toward the building at lunchtime. Faith waved and smiled. Hope waved back.

"Having fun yet?" Faith asked.

"Sure." Hope shrugged. "After all, Joe promised earlier that this was going to be my best summer ever."

Faith laughed. "He loves this place. He grew up here and can't imagine summer without Camp TwinCreeks."

"He sure is into camp." Hope glanced around to see where he was.

As if he could tell he was being talked about, he sidled up and gave Faith a hug. "Sorry I'm all sweaty."

"I know how it is out here. No worries." Faith smiled.

"Well in that case ..." Joe wrapped her up in a bear hug.

"I give. I give!" Faith struggled out of his hold. "You're nothing but a big little boy."

"Eh." He gave a shrug and a grin.

Hope cocked an eyebrow at her sister.

"Joe and Maria are like family to Sam and me. They sort of took us under their wing when we moved down here. So, he's like the brother I never had ... until I married Sam." Faith nudged him with her elbow.

"And she's like the sister I never wanted." Joe mock-punched Faith's arm. Then he looked at Hope. "I guess that makes you my little sister."

For some reason, Hope wasn't okay with that analogy. Why wouldn't she want a brother-sister relationship with Joe? He seemed nice enough. But somewhere deep in her heart she knew it wasn't the kind of friendship she would really like with someone as fun and gorgeous as he seemed to be. Where that thought had come from, she had no idea. She didn't have time for a guy right now. Especially after just breaking up with Kyle. Plus, she wanted nothing to tie her to Texas after this. She was going back to Mississippi as quick as her little Ford could take her.

As Faith and Joe moved on into the building, Hope reminded herself of that again. She did not like Texas. Even if it did have really cute guys.

CHAPTER 7

FAITH

Faith pushed the swing back and forth with one foot while pink began to stretch across the sky. She loved having a westward-facing backyard. The swing was one of the first things she had asked Sam to install when they moved into this house. A breeze swept through her patio and cooled her forehead where the day's heat had not yet dissipated all the way. Cicadas and crickets commenced their evening song.

She tried to figure out what else to include in her latest blog post. After writing so many sad and frustrated posts about barrenness over the years, it was hard to keep from gushing about her elatedness at finally being pregnant. She didn't want this blog to become a hindrance for anyone else who hadn't reached this step in their infertility battle.

Besides getting excited about getting some color on the walls of the baby's room soon, no other news on that front.

In the meantime, my sister is here for the summer. She and I don't always see eye to eye, as is probably the case with most siblings. But we haven't had to live together in years, either, so this is definitely a test in patience for both of us. I'm putting my best foot forward, hoping our relationship can finally reach that stage everyone tells you will happen "one day." You know? "One day, you two will be best friends. Just wait and see." I've heard it all my life. From my lips to your ears, Lord.

The door opened, and Hope came out.

"How was the cookout?" Faith scooted over so her sister could join her.

"It was okay. I found out I'm going to be a fourth-grade girls' counselor starting tomorrow." Hope sat on the far side and leaned against the chains. She studied the sunset as well.

"Tired?" Faith asked.

"A bit. This heat will wear you out." Hope fanned herself with her hand.

"Yes. I always slept really well after I worked at camp all day." Faith stretched her legs out for a moment to make sure her ankles weren't swelling.

"I don't understand how you can stand the heat here." Hope shook her head. "It seems like the sun is so much closer or something."

"We're maybe a little closer to the equator." Faith held her finger and thumb slightly apart from each other. "But not that much. And at least the heat here is more of a dry heat, like being in an oven. Back in Tennessee, it seems like when you walk outside, you have to wade through the humidity to get anywhere."

"I like the humidity."

"It definitely did nothing for my hair." Faith laughed. She refused to give in and argue with her sister tonight. She wanted to just relax on her porch and enjoy the beautiful colors God was painting on the sky.

They were both quiet for a while, each lost in her own thoughts. Faith sighed and absent-mindedly caressed her abdomen where she knew the baby was growing. She had gotten to hear the heartbeat at her last visit, and it was the most beautiful sound she had ever heard in her whole life. She smiled and closed her eyes as she thought back on that moment.

"What does it feel like?" Hope asked.

Faith opened her eyes and met her sister's stare. "What does what feel like?"

"Being pregnant. Is it weird knowing someone is growing inside of you?"

Faith shook her head. "It's the most amazing feeling in the world. I'm finally pregnant, and I love it, even with the little bit of morning sickness I've had and the mood swings and pimples. Knowing that we're finally going to have a baby, someone who will be a little bit of both of us ... it's overwhelming."

"What do you mean *finally*?" Hope cocked her head to one side. "You've only been married a few years."

"Six years and ten months." Faith pointed at her sister. "You were in the wedding. Remember?"

"Yes. I had to wear that horrible blue dress." Hope made a face.

"I'm sure you'll put me in something just as awful when you get married." Faith rolled her eyes. "Besides, it wasn't that bad."

"It made me look like I was three!"

Faith just shook her head.

"It's really been six years?" Hope asked after several more moments.

Faith nodded. The sky was turning more blue and purple than pink now. Just a splash of bright yellow and deep orange lay at the end, as if to fight against the darkness coming over the house to meet it.

"I guess Mom doesn't talk to you, either."

"What does that mean?" Hope turned to face Faith.

Faith took a deep breath and then looked at her sister. "We've been trying to get pregnant for four years now. Mom knew about everything we've gone through ... all the tests and drugs and procedures. But she didn't share with me that she'd gone through a lot of the same until the other day when she found out it had finally worked."

"Faith, I had no idea." A frown marred Hope's forehead.

"Sam and I decided to try and not make a huge deal out of it. We didn't want to be the kind of couple who no one knows how to act around. Afraid they might say something about kids or parenting or anything like that and inadvertently hurt our feelings. We told our parents and a few close friends and God. That's it. It's a very personal struggle we didn't feel like everyone in the world needed to bear with us."

"But at least I could have prayed or something." Hope flopped her hands on her lap.

"I did send you an invite to follow my blog when I started keeping it several years ago." Faith glanced sideways.

"A blog isn't the same thing as my sister telling me in person. I shouldn't have to read it on the internet or hear it from Mom." Hope crossed her arms.

Faith remained silent. A sprinkling of stars shimmered in the sky. She looked at them, looked for lightning bugs, looked anywhere but at Hope. She gently rocked the swing back and forth with her foot.

"Mom went through stuff like that, too?" Hope broke the silence.

"That's what she said. She also miscarried a couple of times. We could have had more siblings if she hadn't had so much trouble." Faith's voice cracked. Just the thought of miscarrying brought a surge of sadness, and she had never even had to go through that.

"Wonder what that means for me in the future." Hope leaned her head back against the floral cushion.

"I think you should worry about getting married first." Faith poked Hope's knee. "What happened with Kyle?"

Hope stood up with a sigh and the swing pitched back and forth out of rhythm for a few seconds. "He was everything Mom said he was. Basically, he didn't want to grow up, didn't know what he wanted to do with his life, didn't have a plan for the future, didn't ever want to get married. I decided I was wasting my time and broke up with him that night after I lost my job and my car."

"Wow, Hopey." Faith used their old nickname. "I'm sorry."

"Don't be sorry over Kyle. He wasn't worth it. And I'll get

another job. And I've got another car. Life goes on." But Hope's voice didn't sound convinced that anything would go as smoothly as she had just stated it would.

"It will work out, and you'll wonder why you ever doubted it would be as great as it will be." Faith reached out and gave a playful tug on Hope's hand.

"You can say that because your life is going exactly how you wanted it to." Hope spun around to face her sister. "You have the husband, the house, the job you love, and now a baby on the way. Of course, you believe it could all happen."

"Hope—"

But it was too late.

Her sister had already stormed into the house and slammed the sliding door behind her. Faith leaned back into the swing and rocked it with her foot again. Her sister was wrong ... if her life had been the way she wanted it exactly, she wouldn't have just a baby on the way, she'd also have a two- or three-year-old, too. Hadn't she just told Hope about how it had taken four years and tons of prayers and medical intervention to be able to get to this point?

She had known something was wrong with Hope but hadn't been able to put a finger on it. Was she actually jealous of Faith's life—the life that Hope had always been quick to criticize and ridicule? Faith shook her head. She wanted a better relationship with Hope, had thought they might be working towards that as they had chatted this evening. Had even wondered if the prayerful blog post she composed in her head earlier had worked with such immediacy. Before the violent outburst. She wanted them to have the kind of bond where they could have real heart-to-hearts with each other instead of every conversation getting their hackles up and ending with pain. A friendship, even.

But now wasn't the time to go into all of that. She and her sister were just getting reacquainted, just catching up with each other. They could delve deeper into dreams and wishes later ... if they were still talking.

CHAPTER 8

HOPE

Hope took a deep breath as she drove to camp early the next morning. Butterflies waged war in her stomach. Even though she had met most of the other staff the day before, she was still nervous about how this would all go. Not that she would ever admit such to her sister.

Faith had reminded her to take sunscreen, water bottle, and swimsuit again this morning, even though she looked rather green as she did it. Hope assumed morning sickness had hit Faith harder this morning than it had the last few. Everything Faith had told her last night about how much she had suffered to get to this place still had Hope reeling. She could sense her sister's pain, could see the tears from the past and get an idea of what all Faith had gone through. And it scared her.

When had she and Faith grown so far apart that her sister deemed her unworthy to know about struggles and problems in her life? And what did it mean for her in the future whenever she finally found Mr. Right and wanted to start a family of her own? She shook the selfish thought out of her head. Both her mom and sister had been able to get pregnant, so there was still hope, unless she never found Mr. Right and then she didn't have to worry about it anyway.

An image of Joe Hernandez popped into her head. She raised an eyebrow at herself. She had just met the guy. Why was he already creeping into her thoughts whenever she considered who Mr. Right might be?

She turned onto the camp property and followed the back path around to the field where the counselors parked. Her car bumped and jostled as she drove through old car tracks from many past years of people parking here. She pulled in between a truck and an SUV—was that seriously all people in Texas drove?

She gathered her bag of extra sunscreen, swimsuit, and lunch and started walking back toward the main area of camp. It was still cool, and she appreciated the breeze that blew her ponytail off the back of her neck. She greeted several of the other counselors as she walked past the benches in front of the main building and entered the office to stash her belongings in her cubbyhole. The board showed she was paired up with a girl named Tessa to be in charge of fourth-grade girls.

Maria came out from an office in the back that belonged to Gran Aunty, as the kids all called one of the owners and founders of the camp. "How are you this morning, Hope?"

"I'm okay." Hope gave Maria a smile. "Not looking forward to how hot it's supposed to get this afternoon, though."

"The first week is always hardest." Maria waved her hand in the air. "Then, you just get used to it. It's nice that you can adjust to it as it heats up during the day. At least it's not as hot from the very beginning as it will be this afternoon."

Hope nodded. "Can you remind me what Tessa looks like? She's my co-counselor, and I can't remember which one she is."

Maria glanced out the front window. "She may be one of the ones on a bus this morning, Hope. She has long brown hair and is just a bit taller than you. But I don't see her here yet."

Hope grabbed the clipboard for her girls. She went out front and started prepping what she would need to have ready for when the kids arrived. Every morning, the campers were dropped off at several different locations in the area and then rode a bus in the rest of the way, singing silly songs and talking to friends. It was easier on the parents that way, as some of the kids lived almost an hour from the camp.

Before any of the counselors were totally ready, the first bus arrived with the kids all singing at the top of their lungs, the song blaring through the open windows. They filed out of the bus, every shape and size. The counselors lined up and gave high fives and steered them in the right direction to get to their groups' meeting places. Hope gathered the basket for the lunchboxes and headed out to the gazebo, where the girls were starting to congregate. Several other buses pulled in, and she spied Joe driving one. He waved at her, and she waved back.

The rest of the girls trickled in as well as Tessa, whom Hope did remember once she saw her. They checked everyone in and found that all eighteen of their girls were present this week. After collecting lunch boxes and lunch money, Tessa walked the basket and clipboard back to the office, where the lunches would stay cool in the air conditioning.

Hope looked at the girls all piled into the gazebo—almost too many to fit the small structure—and wondered what to do next. They were all supposed to be getting to know each other and learning each other's names, but suddenly, all her teacher skills had vanished. She listened to the chatter around her, who had siblings here or who had been here how many times in the past. Some of the girls had been coming to this camp since they were four, and this was their sixth year.

Tessa jumped into the gazebo with a kickball in her hand. "Okay, everyone in a line."

The girls meandered their way into what resembled a line stretching out of the gazebo and then followed Tessa out into the middle of a field. "We're going to play a game. Here are the rules. Everyone has to go around and say their name first. Then, we're going to start throwing a ball back and forth. If you catch the ball, you have to say the name of the girl who threw it. If you can't remember, she will tell you her name again, but you're out and have to sit down. Last one in gets a free snack."

After several rounds, most of the girls seemed to have all eighteen of the names down. Hope thought she could recollect most of them, too. She and Tessa pointed out where things were on campus and then laid out the rules for the week—things like no hitting, don't be mean, stay with the group, get water frequently. Then they took a water break and got ready for the first snack time.

As the girls ran to get their cards punched to mark that they had received their first snack of the day, Tessa and Hope relaxed in the rare moment of quiet in the gazebo.

"How do you like it so far?" Tessa asked.

"It's sort of crazy, but I think it'll be fun. The girls seem like they're going to be great to work with, even though I'm more used to older kids." Hope gave a little shrug. "I teach high school math."

"Wow. I could never do that, but I'm an elementary ed major, so this is a great way to get a taste of what's to come." Tessa laughed. She collected the cards as the girls came back with their bags of pretzels and fruit snacks and bottles of juice or flavored water.

The next session went faster than the first as they showed the girls how to shoot a bow and arrow in archery, something Hope had learned to do only the day before. It wasn't nearly as easy as the movies made it look. She groaned as her arrow flopped to the earth halfway to the target.

"Do as I say and not as I do." She turned to the camper she was trying to demonstrate for and handed off the bow. "Because I am obviously not good at this."

She glanced quickly around and was relieved that no other groups were in sight. How embarrassing would it be for Joe to see her fail so early in the day? Wait—why was he in her head again?

Arts and crafts time came next. They started friendship bracelets, everyone a tangle of embroidery thread and safety pins by the end of the forty-five minutes. She helped them all stash their messes in plastic bags marked with their names so they could try again Thursday.

Lunch time was chaotic but fun. Hope opened her lunchbox to find a note from her sister: "Put on more sunscreen ... trust me. You'll appreciate it later!" Hope rolled her eyes, but did as the note demanded. She hated to admit it, but her sister had a good point. She lathered on the sunscreen before rousting the girls to be on their way to Sing-along.

Despite the old adage of waiting an hour after eating before you swim, the girls had swim lessons next. Hope sat on the side of the pool and cooled her already tired feet in the water as the lifeguards showed the girls how to do the breaststroke. So far, this was Hope's favorite part of the day.

Next came horseback riding lessons, something Hope had no desire to participate in. Up close, those animals were huge, and she was glad to be the counselor to hang out with the girls waiting for their turn on the bleachers instead of the one leading horses from the back wall and helping girls up onto their backs. Maybe by the end of the week she could work up the nerve to get closer, but for now, she'd rather stay right where she was.

After a pitiful game of kickball—these girls seriously didn't want to be out on the hot field running bases this afternoon—they got to enjoy a whole hour of free swim. Before Hope knew it, they were hurrying the girls through the dressing room and gathering up lunchboxes to send them home again. As the last bus drove away, Hope leaned against a wall with her bag on her shoulder.

"You survived the first day." Maria patted her arm.

"Yes." Hope made a face. "It was fun. But I feel so gross right now."

"Well, like the temperatures, you get used to that, too." Maria laughed. "Go home and take a shower. It will make you feel much better."

Hope drove to Faith's house with the air conditioner blowing full blast at her, but she was still soaked with sweat when she arrived.

She grabbed her bag and headed inside with the key Faith had given her. Faith looked up from the table, where she was deep into stamps and scrapbook paper.

"Hey. How was your first day?" She motioned toward the kitchen. "There's cold water in the fridge and cookies on the counter if you're starving."

Hope paused long enough to say, "First, I really need a shower."

Faith laughed. "Go for it. I remember."

Hope stood under the lukewarm water and let it soak through to the deepest and most tired parts of her body. Really, her day had been fun, maybe even more so than she had thought it would. The time after lunch when the kids all gathered and sang silly songs with the counselors and had funny competitions had been a hilarious experience. She couldn't remember the last time she had laughed as hard as she had when some of the boys got up to sing "The Princess Pat."

Joe definitely had all the wiggles down that went with that song. She giggled again as she remembered him pursing his lips to be more girly as he pretended to be a princess. All of the girls at camp, campers and counselors alike, seemed to be in love with him and she could see why. He was one of those people who lit up a room just by walking into it.

Her co-counselor, Tessa, had been fun to work with, too, Hope decided as she dried her hair. She had enough control over the kids to be in charge, but also enough fun moments to really click with the girls and be a great example for them to have. Hope hoped she got to work with Tessa for more than just this week.

She was quiet at the dinner table that night. It wasn't that she didn't have anything to say—she just didn't feel like talking. Faith asked her several questions, and she answered them but didn't offer any elaborations. She caught Faith studying her several times during the meal as well as exchanging worried looks with Sam.

Hope pushed away from the table. "I'm beat. This Texas heat will really suck it out of you. I think I'll just go read for a while and then turn in early."

Sam nodded, and Faith looked like she wanted to object, but then she said, "Sure, Hope. Let us know if you need anything."

Hope pulled the internet up on her laptop and leaned against the headboard. She quickly skimmed her email and then clicked on the bookmarked site that posted job listings in the Oxford area. A glance showed no new math teacher positions. She closed the computer and set it aside. How on earth was this supposed to work? Sure, the camp job wasn't as bad as she had originally expected, but she was so far from where she needed to be right now.

"Come on, God. What is the point of this? I need a job in Mississippi, back where my home is. Not here where it's so hot and flat and barren." She ran a hand through her hair. Sure, it was still early, not even June until the end of the week. Some schools probably hadn't even recovered from the school year enough to know what they needed for the coming one yet. But still … finding a job sooner would be much better than having to wait until later. "Please, God."

~

THE REST of Hope's week went the same way with the addition of joining Sam and Faith Wednesday night for Bible study. Joe dragged her out of Faith and Sam's class to attend the class he was leading. It was a slightly younger group, more singles and college kids than married families.

"It's not that their class is bad, necessarily." He made a silly face. "I just think you'll fit better with this age group."

"Um, how much age difference do you think there is between me and Faith?" Hope asked.

"Okay, so more like … um … where you are in life right now versus where they are in life. I mean we've both been out of college a few years now, but we're not like Faith and Sam, who are married and settled down and expecting a baby. Different place in life."

"I knew what you meant, Joe. I was just teasing."

He grinned at her. "That's okay. I still think you'll like this class. We're studying James."

Joe started the class by reading from James chapter 1. "My brethren, count it all joy when you fall into various trials, knowing that the testing of your faith produces patience. But let patience have its perfect work, that you may be perfect and complete, lacking nothing. If any of you lacks wisdom, let him ask of God, who gives to all liberally and without reproach, and it will be given to him. But let him ask in faith, with no doubting, for he who doubts is like a wave of the sea driven and tossed by the wind. For let not that man suppose that he will receive anything from the Lord; he is a double-minded man, unstable in all his ways."

Hope almost wished she had stayed in Faith's class. She didn't want to "count it all joy" to go through trials. Where was the delight in losing a job and a boyfriend and a car and having to leave her state all in the same day? She refused to see any good in that.

CHAPTER 9

FAITH

"Hope, rise and shine! It's after ten, and as soon as I get back from the store, I'm going to start painting that room." Faith knocked on the door. She heard a moan and some thumps from the other side and assumed her sister was getting up. She walked back toward the kitchen, kissed Sam, and headed to the hardware store.

She knew exactly what color paint she wanted to do the nursery in. She had pretty much known how she wanted it to look, boy or girl, since she was a little girl. The walls would be a pale green, almost a mint, but a little warmer. If it was a boy, she wanted to have things like paper airplane vinyl clings and baseball paraphernalia and trucks and cars and boy things like that. If it was a girl, she wanted to do butterflies and paint some puppies and kitties on the wall.

She also wanted to paint the ceiling to look like the sky with clouds. Then she'd use glow-in-the dark paint to add stars for when their child was going to sleep, but Sam had nixed that idea for now. He said he would have to figure out what to do with the popcorn texture first, which would be a lot more work than they could afford to do at this juncture. She strolled through the aisles, breathing in the smell of oils and wood. It reminded her of her Daddy's garage and going in there to hang out with him while he worked on honey-do projects for her mom. And was evidently one of the few smells that didn't turn her stomach at this point.

Her fingers skimmed the paint chips, looking for the right color. She had picked out some before to show Sam, just to make sure he was on board with her ideas, but she had somehow lost those particular ones. After holding up three or four different sets of green, she finally found one called "Homestead Resort Spa Green," which was the perfect blend, not to yellow or blue. It was light enough to be neutral yet dark enough to show up. She took the chip up to the man behind the counter and had him mix up several buckets.

Maysie met her back at the house. "I left Kendra at home since I figured she would be more of a hindrance than a help."

"We would have put her to work doing something, I'm sure." Faith hugged her.

Maysie took the paint out of Faith's trunk and motioned her on before she could protest. Hope sat at the kitchen counter, finishing a bowl of cereal as they came in.

"Hope, this is my friend Maysie. Maysie, my sister, Hope." Faith motioned between the two.

"I saw you across the church building the other day. It's so good to meet you in person." Maysie set the buckets on the counter. "I feel like I know you already because of everything Faith has told me over the years."

Hope glanced at Faith with her eyebrows raised.

"Good things." Faith held her hands up. "Is your stuff pretty much still packed up so we can move everything to the middle of the room and start painting?"

"Mostly. I may have to throw a few things back in a bag." Hope pointed at Faith. "Aren't paint fumes bad for the baby?"

"I got the kind that's supposed to have way less, and we're going to have the window open in there—sorry if it's a little warmer in there than usual tonight." Faith waved her hand in the air. "We'll be fine."

"Pregnant women paint nurseries all the time." Maysie nodded. "I was much farther along with Kendra when I did her room. But I didn't have a neutral color picked out like your sister does, so I had to wait until I knew if I was having a girl or boy. Her room is very pink."

"What color are you going with?" Hope examined the tops of the buckets. "Green?"

"I love green." Faith hugged one of the pails to her. "It's such a great color for boys or girls."

"If you say so." Hope shrugged.

"Come on. Let's get started." Faith grabbed a bucket and the bag of supplies and walked down the hall. Sam came in and moved the bed and dresser around with Maysie while Faith directed. He had told her she was not to move a single piece of furniture or he wouldn't let her paint at all.

She sat on the edge of the bed and imagined what the walls were going to look like covered in Homestead Resort Spa Green. She opened the packet of paintbrushes and rollers, got out a pan to pour the paint in, and started unfolding a drip cloth to cover the carpet. Hope had been set to taping up the trim so that it would stay white.

"This is going to be so pretty, Faith." Maysie poured the paint into the pan. "I love it."

"I was trying to get her to go with yellow, but she had her heart set on green." Sam rolled his eyes.

"Which you decided you liked after all." Faith bumped her hip into his.

Faith handed Hope a paintbrush, and the two sisters started cutting in the corners and edges while Sam and Maysie worked opposite walls with the rollers. Just over an hour later, they had the first coat on and drying, with the window open and a fan blowing fresh air in from the rest of the house.

"It may be the kind with less fumes, but it still stinks a bit." Hope wrinkled her nose.

"Maybe it won't be as bad after lunch." Faith would never admit the smell was getting to her, too.

Maysie hugged Faith. "I better go. Philip has other things to do this afternoon and someone has to be with the two-year-old."

"Thanks so much for your help."

"Of course. And don't forget I'm planning the baby shower in a few months!" Maysie gave a huge smile before heading out to her minivan.

"She's been wanting to be the one to throw my shower ever since she found out we were trying." Faith laid out sandwich fixings in the kitchen.

"So, she knew this whole time what you were going through, but you didn't feel like you could tell your own sister?" Hope perched on a stool at the counter.

Faith straightened from where she had been digging in the refrigerator. "She's my best friend."

"So that makes her closer than blood?"

"Hope, I told you the other day that we didn't tell many people at all. We didn't want to burden others with our problems. Maysie could see that something was wrong ... she saw me crying in church on Easter and Mother's Day. She saw me quit going to baby showers or sneak away whenever our friends started 'mom' talk. She confronted me to find out what was wrong and wouldn't give up until I told her." Faith planted her hands in front of her sister on the island. "It's not that I wanted to tell her. It just happened because she's around me all the time."

Hope didn't look all the way convinced, but she didn't argue any further, either. Lunch was fairly quiet as they munched on sandwiches and chips. Sam kissed Faith on the forehead and then went into the den to catch a few minutes of the baseball game on television. He had grown up in Texas, so it was pretty much in his blood to root for the Rangers and only them.

"Ready to help with a second coat?" Faith asked as she finished a pickle.

Hope shrugged. "Don't really have a choice, do I?"

Faith opened her mouth to send a nasty reply back, but then thought better of it and shrugged. "It's up to you, but it would probably go faster and therefore be more likely to be dry by tonight if you helped."

Hope gave a short sigh and then followed her sister down the hallway again.

"Coming Sam?" Faith asked as they passed the living room.

"Be right there." He didn't turn from his game, but she knew he would probably get up once it went to a commercial again.

"It looks like it dried pretty well, but paint always looks better with two coats." Faith examined their earlier work. The room was stuffy with the window open, and Faith cranked the ceiling fan up as high as it would go, rolled her sleeves up, and picked up a paintbrush to get back to work. Sam joined them within a few minutes and started rolling again.

"The boys are looking good this year." He was talking about his baseball game.

"That's good. Maybe we can sneak up to Arlington for a game." Faith glanced over her shoulder. "We'll just have to check their home schedule against our schedule, but we're fairly open during the summer. I bet Chrissy and John would let us stay with them."

"We haven't seen them in several years." Sam poured more paint in the pan.

"Our cousin Chrissy?" Hope asked.

"Yeah." Faith took a damp towel and wiped at a spot on the window sill that had received a drip of green. "They live in the Dallas area. Every now and then, we'll meet up with them around Waco and spend a day, but we haven't found the time in a while."

"What does John do again?" Hope stepped up on a ladder and worked at a spot in the far corner.

"What everyone in this family seems to do." Sam laughed. "He's a teacher."

"Oh!" Faith stood up and looked across the room at Hope. "That reminds me."

Hope paused in her painting and regarded Faith. "Of?"

"One of our friends at church works at the school district in one of the other towns in the area. She knew you were looking for a job and wanted me to tell you there's a job fair there in a couple weeks. She knows there are going to be several math positions open and said to just give her a call if you have any questions."

Hope clenched her jaw as if she were trying not to say something she would regret.

Sam glanced over his shoulder as the silence hung heavy in the room.

"Did Mom ask you to do that?" Hope finally asked.

"Do what?" Faith glanced over her shoulder from where she had gone back to work.

"Mom had this crazy idea that Texas was the only state in the union looking for teachers right now. That's one of the reasons she wanted me to move out here. For some reason, she just has this thing against me living in Mississippi. I don't know why." Hope threw her paintbrush in the bucket of water and stood up. "But I won't move to Texas long-term. I belong in Mississippi, no matter what Mom thinks."

"Hope, it was just someone trying to be helpful. Have you heard of any openings in Mississippi? If you have, by all means, we're not going to stop you from moving back." Faith held her hands up as if to wave a white flag.

"It's sort of hard to hear of things when you're two states away." Hope pointed in a direction that was nowhere near east, but Faith wasn't about to mention that.

Instead, Faith let a sigh slip through her lips.

Hope glared at her. "It's not like I don't have a life and can just up and move wherever you guys think I should. I do have a life. I have a roommate expecting me to come back this fall and share rent. And I have friends and a church family in Oxford. And we were going to go to an Ole Miss football game this fall and root on our Rebels. I am not going to stay in Texas one day longer than I absolutely have to."

"And with an attitude like that, we don't want you to." Sam's comment was just loud enough for everyone to hear.

"Sam!" Faith jerked her attention to him.

Hope pushed past Faith and out the door. Faith went after her, but by the time she caught up, Hope was getting in her car.

"Hope, let's talk about this." Faith caught the door before Hope could shut it. "I'm not trying to force you to move to Texas."

"I don't want to talk about it. I'll be back later."

"Where are you going?" Faith asked, but Hope wrenched the car door out of Faith's hands and slammed it without answering. She backed out of the driveway so fast that she almost hit the mailbox across the street. Faith stood there until Hope passed the point where Faith couldn't see her anymore, then went back into the kitchen and poured herself a cup of water.

"Where'd she go?" Sam asked.

"I don't know." Faith took a drink. "She drove off without answering that question."

"I told you it was a bad idea to let her come this summer. Now you're getting stressed out, and that's not good for the baby."

"Sam, you're not helping." She slammed her cup on the counter, water sloshing over her hand. She bent over and wrapped her arms around herself. "I'm sorry."

He pulled her up and cradled her against his chest. He reeked of paint and sweat. She leaned further into his hug anyway, enjoying the way his arms felt around her.

"I just wanted to help her. I had no idea she would have such a reaction." Faith sobbed into his shirt.

"I know, honey." He stroked her hair and rocked her in a gentle back-and-forth sway. "I know."

Her phone jangled, and she quickly plucked it from her pocket with hopes it was her sister. Instead, the word *Mom* flashed across the screen. She handed it to Sam.

"You answer it. I don't know what to tell her."

"Hannah?" Sam leaned back against the counter and gave her a look. "Yeah, she's a little upset right now."

That was an understatement. She walked back down the hallway to try to paint some more. She was angry, hurt, frustrated, and tired. *Upset* just didn't seem to reach where she was. But she was also worried about her sister.

It seemed like everything she had said today had sparked some sort of anger or hurt in her sister. Was their relationship just doomed to be like this forever? How on earth was she going to be able to let Hope be an aunt to this baby if she couldn't keep from yelling and arguing every time they got together? It wasn't a healthy way to live. If only Hope would talk to her instead of letting everything simmer underneath until it boiled up like this afternoon.

She looked at the picture of the two of them as girls again, wishing their lives were still as peaceful. Maybe she should look for a field of wildflowers somewhere. If they went and sat amid God's beauty, could they somehow find their way back to that relationship?

CHAPTER 10

HOPE

Hope didn't set out with a particular destination in mind. She just knew she needed to get out of the house and away from her perfect sister with her perfect life. Her phone buzzed, and a quick glance told her Mom was trying to call. She pushed the button on the side of the phone until the device powered off. She might have to pay for it later, but right now she had no desire to talk to anyone in her family.

As if her life weren't hard enough, everyone kept trying to complicate it more. First, her mom convinced her to move two states away from where she wanted to be. Now, her sister had joined forces with Mom and pushed this job fair which would only get her a job here instead of in the state she was supposed to be living in. Just because there still weren't any jobs available around Oxford—and she checked at least twice a day—it didn't mean she was about to give up. Would Mom or Faith give up if one of their dreams didn't seem possible? She huffed.

Okay, maybe that was a little unfair. Because lo and behold, both of them had had to struggle to achieve their dreams of being mothers. Not that they had mentioned any of this to her until lately. But still ... now that they had their dreams, shouldn't they support hers even more, knowing what it was like to fight for something you wanted so badly?

Hope pulled off the interstate when she saw a big sign for a bookstore. The quiet chatter, rustle of pages, and smell of paper, ink, and coffee immediately calmed her nerves. She ordered a hot chocolate despite it being over ninety degrees outside. Sometimes a girl needed comfort more than common sense.

She wandered through various sections until she found a book title that sounded interesting. Grabbing the tome, she settled into a nearby chair and skimmed the first few pages to see if it really was as good as the jacket made it out to be. Even though fantasy wasn't a genre she normally read, she got lost enough in it that she jumped when someone knocked into her chair.

She looked up into Joe's dark brown eyes.

"I thought that was you." He pointed to her.

Startled, Hope noticed for the first time how low the sun was in the sky. She must have spent several hours in here, not realizing how much time had passed. She marked her place in the story with her finger and sat up straighter.

"You know they really expect you to buy it before you read the whole thing." He plopped down in the chair next to hers.

"I honestly didn't mean to read more than a few pages just to see if it was any good. Guess it was." She held up the book and realized she had read over a third of it.

"Did Faith kick you out?" He plucked the paperback from her hands to see the cover.

"No. I guess I sort of ran away."

He looked up with skepticism written in his expression.

"We may or may not have gotten in a fight this afternoon." Hope glanced down at her hands.

"Over what?" Joe asked. "Or am I being too nosy?"

"You are being too nosy." She wrinkled her nose at him. "But I'll tell you anyway because you're one of the only friends I have here."

He put his hands over his heart and batted his eyelashes. "Aw!"

"Stop it!" A laugh escaped, and a lightness filled her for the first time all day.

"So, how about I treat you to dinner while you tell me this horrible tale?" He stood. "I was about to check out, and since you haven't moved since I came in almost an hour ago, I figure you haven't eaten yet, either."

"I don't know." She took the paperback he handed her and replaced it on the shelf. "I should probably get back and apologize."

"So, the fight was your fault?" He playfully bumped her arm.

"No!" Her head came up to meet his gaze, and she realized he hadn't been serious. "No. I just reacted badly."

"Come on." Joe grabbed the novel back off the shelf and led her to the checkout line. "I'll pay for these and we can go get something to eat. I'm starving."

Before she knew what happened, he had purchased the story she had escaped into earlier, pushed her into his old, beat-up Jeep, and they were driving down the road to a burger joint. She leaned back against the leather seats and listened to some country music singer crooning about how he had lost everything he ever loved. People were all around them, but she could only focus on one—the driver of the vehicle she was in.

Once they were settled at a table covered in red-checked cloth with their orders placed, he looked at her again. "So, about this fight. Did you give her a bloody nose?"

"Maybe *argument* would be a better word."

"Okay. I've known Faith for about five years now. She is one of the sweetest people I've ever met, and I have no idea how Sam got so lucky as to catch her eye. What on earth could she have done to tick you off so much?" He played with his straw paper, wrinkling and flattening it out.

Hope sighed. "She suggested I go check out a job fair."

"I see." Joe nodded. "You don't want to work. I would be mad, too."

"Stop that!" She swatted at him. "You're putting words in my mouth. It's not that I don't want to find a job. It's that I don't want a job here, in Texas. I live in Mississippi."

"What if you can't find a job in Mississippi?"

She glared at him. "I don't know."

"So, you're keeping your options open. Good."

"Joe, what if someone suggested you go find a job somewhere else? What if you had to quit being an associate minister or camp counselor, leave your beloved state of Texas, and go live in another state? Would you be happy about it?" Hope raised an eyebrow.

"Actually," he said after taking a sip of soda, "I'm considering moving."

Hope leaned back against her seat. "Really?"

"That's the plan." He shrugged. "I'm thinking of going down to work in Honduras for a few years as a missionary."

"That's great, Joe." Hope shook her head. "I had no idea."

"My mom doesn't know, either. I haven't figured out how to tell her. I know I need to do it soon, but it's so hard. Since my father died, I'm all she has left. Who knows the next time she'll get to see me if I'm in a whole other country?"

"But it's your choice, Joe." Hope leaned forward and grabbed his hands. He looked up at her, and she realized what she had done. She quickly let go again and scooted back.

"It's my choice? Yes." He tapped his finger on the table. "But that doesn't mean it's going to be easy. It was your choice to move here this summer, too, but I get the feeling it wasn't easy for you, either. That doesn't mean it can't be great in the end, though. I'm looking forward to the work in Honduras, to helping those people who appreciate the little things so much more because it's all they have. And your summer doesn't have to be horrible either, even if it was a hard choice to make. You just have to look for the good with the bad."

Her choice to move here? Yes. In a way, it had been her choice. In another way ... she mentally shook her head. Joe obviously hadn't met her mother. When Mom got an idea in her head, she was relentless until she made it happen.

And just because Joe had reminded Hope that her summer didn't have to be bad even though she didn't really want to be here, it didn't change the fact that she wanted to live in Mississippi again, not in Texas. This was supposed to be an interim thing, a means to an end. Going to that job fair would admit defeat, and she wasn't quite to that point yet. It was still early. Right?

The rest of dinner was quiet as Joe let Hope remain in her thoughts. He dropped her off and then waited until she was on the road before he pulled out of the parking lot, too. She waited in the driveway a few extra minutes after pulling in, trying to work up the nerve to go inside.

She opened the door as quietly as possible, not sure what to expect. The television was on in the living room with Sam in front of it. He got up when he saw her in the doorway. She flinched at the look in his eyes.

"I know you're going through a lot, Hope. We both know that. We've tried to make it as easy as we could for you this summer, but you're not exactly making it easy for us to do that. Faith has bent over backwards to make sure everything would go well for you, and if this is how you're going to repay her, then you can just go back to your beloved Mississippi."

Hope opened her mouth to say something and then closed it again.

Sam took the opportunity to continue. "This may not be your idea of what a perfect summer is. You may not like the way the weather is here or that you're having to sweat every day to earn a few extra dollars. But in the end, this was your choice. Yes, your mom suggested it, but you could have said, 'No.' You didn't, and you're here. Of your own free will. So, even if you don't like it, deal with it. Because it was your choice."

Hope blinked at the similarity of what Sam said and what Joe had told her earlier. It was the theme tonight, pointing out that this summer had been her decision in the end. She remained skeptical, but everyone else seemed to be convinced.

"And the next time you feel like yelling at someone, pick someone other than my wife. She spent the whole afternoon worrying about you, wondering where you had gone and how she could make it right. And then when your mom called back and said you weren't answering your phone, that just made it worse. She basically made herself sick, put you first instead of her health and the baby. The baby we have yearned for now for almost five years. And I am not okay with that. So, please, at least while in this house, think about your actions and the consequences they'll have on other people." Sam turned his back on her and went back to his recliner.

Hope just nodded once and continued her walk down the hallway. She paused at Faith's bedroom door. It was open a crack, and she could see her sister inside, sleeping even though the light was on.

"I'm sorry, Faith." She whispered, not wanting to wake her sister.

Faith stirred anyway and looked at the door. "Hope?"

"I'm sorry, Faith." Hope repeated the words, louder this time.

Faith sat up and opened her arms. "I'm sorry, too."

Hope went in and hugged Faith and then sat on the edge of the bed. "I overreacted."

"But I knew you were unhappy here, and I pushed you anyway." Faith touched Hope's arm.

Hope shook her head. "Joe pointed out that it was my choice to move here. So did Sam, when I came in."

"You were with Joe?"

"He found me at the bookstore and kidnapped me until after dinner." Hope tucked a strand of hair behind her ear. "I really didn't mean to stay gone so long, but I got wrapped up in a novel in the store and lost track of time."

"If you were with Joe, then I had no reason to worry." Faith leaned against the headboard.

"Your husband is pretty ticked at me right now."

Faith glanced through the door as if she could see Sam around the corner. "He'll get over it by morning. He doesn't like to see me unhappy. He's been super overprotective of me ever since we found out I'm pregnant. I keep telling him women have babies every day, but he still thinks he needs to wrap me in bubble wrap or something."

"I hope I can find someone who feels the same about me one day." As Hope made this admission, Joe appeared in her head. She mentally shook herself. He was going to Honduras to be a missionary. She needed to find another perfect guy.

But first, she needed to find a new job. And to make sure she didn't upset her sister anymore while she was staying here. She didn't know how to accomplish either of those things.

"You will." Faith reached over and squeezed her hand. "And, until then, I promise not to push you about job fairs anymore."

Hope let out a small laugh. "And I'll try to not be so—"

"Hopey, just relax. We love you, even if Sam is mad right now. We only wanted to help. There's no pressure on our part for you to stay here if you don't want to." Faith cocked her head to one side. "But I have no say in what Mom suggests when you talk to her. And you need to call her tonight and let her know you're safe. She was more upset than I was."

Hope scrunched up her face. "Yeah, okay." She rose and headed out.

"I'm sorry I didn't let you know about our fertility struggles." Faith's voice caught Hope as she reached the door.

Hope turned back and looked at her sister. "And I'm sorry that our relationship wasn't where it needed to be so that you felt like you could. Love you."

And for the first time in several years, the sentiment came naturally.

Back in her room, Hope reluctantly sat down on the edge of the bed and turned her phone back on. The ceiling fan moved the air around enough that she could handle the remaining fumes and heat. No less than fifteen missed calls and messages from Faith and their mom. She sighed and punched the button to call Mom and reassure her that her kidnapper had been friendly. With a secret smile, she admitted he was better than friendly. *No, Hope. Stop it. Remember what he told you.*

How far was it from Mississippi to Honduras?

She was almost relieved to hear her mom's angry voice over the phone because it meant she couldn't dwell on that insane thought. Not that she wouldn't be counting the hours until she could see him again … at church services the next morning and at camp on Monday.

CHAPTER 11

◈

HOPE

Hope skimmed her finger along the list of who was counseling which group. Her name was not with the fourth-grade girls like she expected it to be. She skimmed through the list again and cocked an eyebrow.

First-grade boys. *Boys*? What was she supposed to do with boys? And first graders, no less.

"I see you're with Joe this week." Maria appeared beside her.

"I'm not sure I know what to do with first-grade boys. I was pushing my limits just by working with fourth-grade girls." Hope tugged at the end of her French braid. "I usually deal with high school kids, not ... kids just out of kindergarten!"

"You'll do great. Mostly, you're there to help Joe. He's been their counselor for several years now, and he loves it."

"Here goes nothing." Hope gave a shrug.

The guys new to camp were fairly quiet as they filed into the first-grade boy's cubby, a small pavilion with benches around the edge, all painted red. The ones who had been to camp last week and knew each other were boisterous, dropping their lunchboxes into the basket or checking out each other's new swim goggles. Hope somehow had most of them checked in by the time Joe appeared after dropping off his bus.

"Good morning." His voice was sing-songy yet loud enough to be heard over the cacophony.

"Hey, Mr. Joe!" Several of the kids gave him high fives.

Hope scooted over as much as she could without smooshing a child and made room for Joe beside her. He sat down and went through the pages to go over names and allergies. His leg pressed against hers, making it hard to concentrate on the little boys more than the big one next to her.

"Okay, guys, listen up." Joe set the clipboard aside and clapped his hands. "We've got some ground rules here at Camp TwinCreeks. Does anyone who's been here before know what some of them are?"

Several hands shot up, but one cotton-top just stood up and said, "No throwing rocks or sticks."

Hope grinned.

"Right." Joe nodded. "That's a good rule. What else?"

"No yelling or running at horseback."

"No running at the swimming pool."

"Only one snack at each snack time."

"Don't be mean."

"Those are all great rules." Joe gave a thumbs up. "What about listening to your counselors? Do you think you should do that?"

Muttered agreements sounded all around.

"What about when we tell you to get a drink of water? Do you think that might be a good idea?" Joe pointed towards the fountains.

"What if you're not thirsty?" A redhead named Simeon asked.

"Is it going to be hot here today?" Joe raised his eyebrows.

"Yes."

"Then we need to keep lots and lots of water in our bodies because it all goes out when we sweat. I don't know about you, but I sweat when I get hot." Joe hooked a thumb towards her. "Maybe Ms. Hope doesn't sweat much because she's a girl, but we boys are sweaty and gross. So, we need to drink lots of water so we can sweat more, okay?"

Hope shook her head at that repulsive thought. This week was definitely going to be different than the previous one had been. Boys were a lot more into disgusting things than girls.

Although many of the activities were the same, the boys needed another kind of counselor than the girls had the week before. The younger kids liked to have counselors play games with them or watch them do "tricks" in the pool. They were still willing to hold hands every now and then and wanted to sing silly songs at times other than the sing-along after lunch.

"Ms. Hope, look at me." Simeon went underwater and came up again.

"That's great." She sat on the side of the pool next to Joe, both with their shoes off and feet wet. It was still morning, so it hadn't gotten very hot yet, but it still felt good to wiggle her toes in the cool water.

"You're great with the boys." Joe nudged her with his elbow.

"I've only been with them a couple hours so far." She leaned over to splash a boy who had come up to try and tickle her feet. "Maybe you should wait until the end of the day to decide that for sure."

"Nah. You're great."

Great? Was that a reiteration of his earlier statement, or was it a general truth, as in she was great in general? She wasn't about to ask. A dark-haired boy named Mark swam up and grabbed her legs. She kicked them up and down and he let his body float back and forth with the motion. She quit, and he grinned at her.

"Ms. Hope, are you Mr. Joe's girlfriend?" he asked.

Her cheeks were hot from more than just the temperature. She wasn't used to kids who were so straightforward. Especially added to what she had been contemplating only a few moments before.

"She's a girl, and she's my friend." Joe said.

"Okay." Mark swam back to his friends. They could hear him tell them, "She's just his friend and a girl."

The whistle blew for everyone to get out of the pool, but Hope could have sworn she heard, "at least for now," come out of Joe's mouth. She glanced his way, but he was already slipping his shoes back on so he could go let the boys into the dressing room. She followed behind to round up the stragglers. She hurried the last few into the room, telling them as soon as they were dressed they could go get their snacks.

Snack time flew by, and they lined up for crafts. This had become Hope's favorite time of day. And this week, Faith was the one in charge of this activity. Faith's doctor had decided as long as she stayed mostly in the air-conditioned craft building, she could work several weeks of camp. After much jostling and commotion, Joe and Hope got all the boys sitting around the tables. Joe whistled with his finger and thumb between his lips, and everyone quieted and looked toward the front of the room.

"Boys, this is Ms. Faith and she's our crafts counselor this week." Joe pointed between Hope and Faith. "She's also Ms. Hope's sister. Do you think they look like sisters?"

Hope frowned a bit. She had always hated being told that she looked like Faith. Their blonde hair was completely different in shades, with Faith's more of a strawberry and Hope's more like honey. And Faith's nose was more like their mom's, while Hope had inherited her father's larger honker. The boys didn't make many comments about Joe's question, and Faith just shook her head.

"Today, since it's robot week, we're going to design our own robots out of these boxes and buttons and pipe cleaners and things." Faith held up an example. "Each boy will get one box to start with, and then your counselors will bring around some glue for you to use to stick the buttons on how you want them. You need to decide what it should look like before you start gluing anything. Otherwise, you might change your mind, but it won't come off again."

The boys were the quietest Hope had heard them all day as they worked. She went around with a bottle of glue to refill the containers the boys were using as they got low. Joe leaned over, helping a boy curl a pipe cleaner around his finger to make it look like a spring. Hope glanced over at Faith as she sat on a stool in the front of the room. Faith grimaced and rubbed her hand across her abdomen before she noticed Hope watching.

"You okay?" Hope asked quietly when she got back to the front.

"Yeah." Faith gave a half-hearted grin. "I think I just ate something that's disagreeing with the baby."

"You sure?"

"Hope, I'm fine. Go help your boys."

Hope watched her sister out of the corner of her eye the rest of the time they were there and gave her a quick hug before she left. She made herself a mental note to check with her later in the day. She may have never been pregnant before, but she was pretty sure you weren't supposed to hurt enough to make the face Faith had made.

The rest of the day went quickly as they went to horseback, had lunch, did archery—where her arrow thankfully sailed all the way to the target today and did not embarrass her in front of the guys—and played on the playground. They finished up with more swimming and then games with Willie Bob, an older counselor who was a fixture here at camp. He told silly stories and played ridiculous games. This one was called Colored Eggs.

"Now, this is a very sophisticated game." Willie Bob clasped his hands and looked semi-serious.

Several boys giggled.

"Here are the rules. We're going to have a wolf, and we're going to have the rest of you. Joe, you come be the wolf and I'll be everyone else."

Joe cupped his hands around his mouth. "Knock, knock!"

"Who's there?" Willie Bob made his voice higher pitched to mimic the boys'.

"The big bad wolf." Joe's voice got very grumbly. Several boys snickered.

Willie Bob wrung his hands. "What do you want?"

"Colored eggs."

"What color?"

Joe pretended to be thinking about what color he wanted.

Willie Bob wiggled his eyebrows at the campers. The next part was obviously the best. "If the wolf guesses the color wrong, you say, 'Flushed down the toilet.'"

Several of the guys doubled over in laughter at that.

"If the wolf guesses right, you run to that tree and yell and scream because if he catches you, then you have to be a wolf, too. Got it?" Willie Bob asked.

The counselors got to be the wolves first. Willie Bob helped the boys pick a color while Joe and Hope waited with the second-grade-boys' counselors. Finally, the boys lined up with goofy grins on their faces, and they went through the beginning dialogue until they got to the guessing part.

One counselor said, "Green!"

"Flushed down the toilet."

"Purple."

"Flushed down the toilet."

"Red!" Joe cupped his hands around his mouth to be even louder.

"What kind of red?" Some of the boys leaned over as if to get ready to run.

"Apple red." Another counselor shifted her weight.

"Flushed down the toilet."

"Cardinal red." Hope said.

"Flushed down the toilet."

"It wouldn't have anything to do with a mask." Willie Bob winked as he dropped the hint.

"Superhero red!" The counselors yelled together.

The boys hollered and started running. Hope grabbed at several as she chased them across the yard. Despite their legs being so much shorter than hers, she only caught one. She joined the counselors back in the middle for another round, now with five new wolves to help. After several more sets of that game, they moved on to play Tornado, where everyone formed a big *O* and held hands. Then, one person would be the twister in the middle and come racing toward a part of the circle as if to break through. The entire group had to work together to keep the cyclone contained so it didn't escape and destroy the whole camp.

"You coming to Counselor Night tomorrow night?" Joe asked at the end of the day as they handed out lunchboxes and made sure boys got to the right bus.

"Maybe." Hope redirected Simeon as he meandered in the wrong direction.

"You should. It's a lot of fun. We play volleyball and kickball. There's burgers and Gran Aunty's famous banana pudding."

"Maybe," Hope said again, this time with a grin.

"I have all day tomorrow to talk you into it."

∽

Joe did end up talking Hope into coming to Counselor Night. At six Tuesday evening, she found herself strolling up to the main building, even though she had only been gone for a couple of hours. She had taken a shower despite the likelihood of getting dirty again this evening and wore a clean flower-print sleeveless top and blue capris. Tessa was heading out as Hope walked in.

"Come on." Tessa pulled Hope outside and into a golf cart. "We've got to go get some serving spoons from Gran Aunty's." Tess put it in gear, and they drove down the driveway to the back of the campus, where Gran Aunty and Uncle Gramps lived.

After greeting the older couple and getting the utensils, the girls slid back onto the cart, but when Tessa pushed the pedal, nothing happened. She made sure the brake was off and tried reverse, but it still wouldn't budge.

Hope leaned over and studied the panel. "Um, Tess. Is it on?"

Tessa turned the key the other direction and the cart lurched forward. "This is why blondes aren't supposed to drive."

They were still laughing about it when they got back to the main building. The burgers on the grill scented the air with their smoky aroma. Several others were walking in, too. It was strange to see some of them in clothes a bit nicer than what they normally wore to work at camp. No one risked flip-flops, though. Too big of an invitation for chiggers and fire ants.

After eating, they all gathered around the volleyball court, and several broke off into two teams to play. Hope sat on the sidelines, secretly rooting for Joe's team but vocally cheering for Tessa on the other side. As it started to get dark, they all filed to the kickball field and flipped on the lights. The girls challenged the boys, and Hope was up first.

She stepped up to the plate and faced down Charlie, the guy pitching. He brought his arm back a bit and then let the red ball go. It bounced three or four times as it rolled toward her. She pulled her leg back, kicked it forward with all her might, and miraculously redirected the ball toward the space between third and second base. She took off at a mad sprint toward first as the girls cheered her on in the background. Joe was there, his arms waiting to catch the ball, as she neared the base.

Momentum was a cruel force.

Her feet touched the bag, but she couldn't stop. The dirt was slick. Her shoes slid. The world went out from under her.

Maybe an extra-wide step would help?

No such luck. The earth quickly rose to meet her.

At the last second, she tucked her head and rolled as her body collided with the ground. "Oof!"

Could she move? She squeezed her eyes closed tight and then opened them again, the breath slowly refilling her lungs. Her brain scrambled to figure out what was actually hurting, instead of just screaming that her whole body was on fire from the pain.

Joe came into view above her, a worried look on his face. "You okay?"

"I think so." She groaned. "Just catching my breath."

She eased to her feet and took inventory. Grass and dust covered her shoulder and knee. Blood trickled down her leg.

"I think we better go patch you up." Joe said.

"I'm okay." Hope refused to admit how much everything ached at that moment. Could she die of embarrassment?

"At least let's try and keep the blood from staining your socks." He pointed to the red oozing closer to her ankle as she stood there.

She let him lead her off the field and back toward the building. It was dark away from the lights, and she was grateful for his presence and the slight pressure of his hand on the small of her back as they picked their way along the drive. Crickets and frogs sang in the night, mixing their sounds with the cicadas.

Joe sat Hope down in a chair in the nurse's station and wet several paper towels with some antibacterial liquid. With hands as gentle as a butterfly alighting, he patted her scraped knee and got the dirt out of the wound. He held up a bandage with a cartoon character on it and grinned at her.

"Nice kick, by the way."

"Thanks." She laughed. "I guess it didn't do my team much good, since I don't think I'll be doing anymore running tonight."

"Does it hurt much?"

"Mostly my pride."

He grinned up at her. "How's the shoulder?"

She let him examine it. He gently patted another paper towel around the small scrapes there and picked off some grass that was caught at the edge of her tank top. He pushed the strap back a bit and laughed.

"What?" She looked around, trying to see what was so funny.

"You are getting a tan." His finger followed the line where her shirt ended and the sun had actually touched. His hand on her skin sent shivers through her belly. She closed her eyes for a moment, savoring the experience.

"Did that hurt?" He froze.

Her eyes flew open to find his face close to hers. "No."

He helped her stand up again and didn't release her hands right away. She held her breath as he just looked at her, their bodies only inches apart. Finally, he took a step back and let go as they heard other voices outside the building.

She released her breath. Had he been wanting to kiss her? Was she okay with that? At this moment, her heart and brain were in a strong argument, and she wasn't sure which one would win. All she knew was that tonight, for the first time since she had moved here, she wasn't a bit sad that she was single again. Or in Texas.

CHAPTER 12

FAITH

Faith had tried to convince herself all week that the little discomforts and pains she had been experiencing were nothing more than indigestion. She refused to think otherwise. Sam had suggested she call her doctor when the pains persisted through Tuesday, especially when she mentioned she had spotted a bit. The doctor had told her to leave camp, come in for a little blood work, and then go home and rest, just to be on the safe side, since there was still a strong heartbeat. She had stayed in bed from that day through Friday. It was getting worse, though.

Hope looked up from her spot on the sofa as Faith emerged from her bedroom late that afternoon. Faith tried not to grimace as another pain seized her middle, and she headed for the bathroom. She was too scared of what this might mean to want to talk about it with her sister.

Her heart skipped a beat when she saw the blood.

"No, God." Her prayer was no louder than a whisper as she tried to control the sobs that wanted to escape her body. "No."

"Faith?" Hope knocked at the door. "You okay?"

Faith took a deep breath and tried to pull herself together. God was a god of love. He couldn't be this cruel, this mean. To finally let this miracle start growing inside her, only to rip it away again? No.

"Faith?" Hope jiggled the door knob. "Faith, what's going on?"

Faith inched open the door and met her sister's eyes. "I'm bleeding, Hope."

"Did you cut yourself?"

"Hope." Faith put her hands on her sister's shoulders and tried to control the wobble in her voice. "I'm bleeding." She choked back another sob. "I think I'm losing the baby."

Hope looked shocked for a moment and then snapped into action. "Call your doctor and tell him we're on the way. I'm driving. Grab your shoes and let's go. We can call Sam on the way."

Faith stood there for another second as she watched her sister lunge for her own pair of flip flops and grab her purse.

Hope turned around and motioned. "Come on!"

Faith shook her head and then walked back in her room to find her own shoes and her cell phone. She scrolled down the list of numbers until she found the one she was looking for.

"Dr. Wyatt's office," a friendly voice said.

"This is Faith McCreary. I'm ten weeks pregnant. I was in a couple days ago to let you guys know I was spotting, but the bed rest ... I don't think it worked. I'm bleeding. Can you get me in this afternoon?" She squeezed her eyes closed against the threatening tears. "I don't want to lose my baby."

"Okay, Mrs. McCreary." The sound of typing came through the phone. "Can you get here by four-thirty?"

Faith glanced at the kitchen clock as she walked through the house to find her sister. It was already after four. "I'll be there as soon as I can."

Hope zipped through the streets, almost not leaving herself enough time to follow Faith's directions. Faith dialed her husband's number to let him know what was going on.

"Sam." Faith tried to steel her voice when he answered. He was at the church building, getting ready for a lock-in and knew she would be calling only if it was an emergency.

"What's wrong?"

"I'm on my way to the doctor. I'm bleeding. They're going to get me in this afternoon to check things out. It's probably nothing ..." Nothing? This was everything. If only she could wake up and find this all to be a nightmare!

"I'm on my way."

"Don't you have to be there for the lock-in?"

"Faith, I'm your husband first. I'll be there as soon as I can." He paused for a moment. "That's my baby, too. And I love you both."

Faith swiped at a tear and tried to get control of herself. Until anyone said so, this baby was fine and there was no need for tears. She took a deep breath and repeated that to herself.

"Turn here." Faith pointed the driveway out to Hope. They pulled into the parking lot with five minutes to spare.

Faith grabbed her middle as another pain wrapped around her when she stood. If she didn't know better, she would say she was going into early labor. But this was way too early. She was only ten-and-a-half weeks along. They sat in the waiting room fifteen minutes before the nurse came to take her back to the examination room. Hope offered to come back with her, but Faith requested she stay out in the lobby to be there when Sam arrived.

"My husband is on his way." Faith glanced out the window as she met the nurse, hoping against hope that he had made the drive in less time than normal. "Can he come back when he gets here?"

"It will depend." The nurse shut the door, and Faith was pretty sure her heart got slammed in the hinges, as much as it hurt with that statement.

Faith's feet dangled over the edge of the exam table. She studied the ugly picture of water fowl on the wall. She noticed the cracks in the tile floor and how some of the tiles no longer met each other at the edges. She avoided looking at the charts and diagrams of various diseases and problems women could have. She also evaded the sight of the numerous probes and other items physicians used when doing exams. She hated doctors' offices, and she had been in this one too many times over the last few years.

Another half hour passed before Dr. Wyatt finally knocked on the door and came in. "Faith, how are you today?"

Faith hated that question. If she was doing well, she wouldn't be sitting in his office, would she? Although she had to admit deep down the last time she had been here had been a good visit. They had listened to the baby's heartbeat, that beautiful *whump, whump, whump* that she had never wanted to stop.

"I'm bleeding." It sounded so matter-of-fact when she said it, as if it were something she dealt with all the time. As if it weren't the end of the world.

"Well, that could be normal. A lot of women have some bleeding during the pregnancy." He pulled her chart up on the computer to check her blood pressure and see her history.

"I'm also having some cramping. It's almost like what I've heard labor pains are like."

"Well, let's not panic, yet, okay?" He glanced up. "Let's do some bloodwork to check hormone levels, and let's do an ultrasound to see what's going on in there, okay?"

She nodded and then put herself on autopilot as the nurse came in to take blood and handed her the ever-stylish paper gown. She got ready to see her insides on the little gray screen. As the blob came up that was her womb, she noticed it didn't look quite like it had two weeks earlier. There was no movement at all from the tiny little person in the middle of the screen. The flutter the Doppler broadcasted the last time she was in was absent.

"God, please." She prayed under her breath.

The doctor didn't say anything for several minutes as he positioned the equipment several different directions to try and get a picture. Faith quit watching the screen and watched his face instead. She didn't see any hope there. When he turned to face her, she didn't have the courage to ask what she wanted to know. Or what she didn't want to know.

"You get dressed again and we'll talk about this in my office, okay?" He patted her on the knee before he left her in privacy.

Clothed again, she met up with her husband, and they both entered the doctor's office. She held on to Sam's hand as they perched in the two chairs in front of Dr. Wyatt's messy desk. He had several pictures of his own three beautiful children mixed amid the scattered papers and pens and chart folders. Slowly, he met their eyes.

"You're miscarrying," he said bluntly.

Faith could have sworn her heart was beating a moment before, but now she couldn't feel it anymore. Was she going to die, too, right along with her baby? Would God be that cruel? Or that kind?

"Is there any way to stop it?" Sam asked.

"What about progesterone?" Faith found her voice with that small glimmer of hope.

"I'm sorry. But even if we stopped it from happening, it wouldn't do any good. There was no heartbeat." Dr. Wyatt shook his head.

A baby couldn't survive without a heartbeat. Faith's baby was dead already, even though it was still inside her.

Dead.

The hand not clinging to Sam gripped the edge of the chair. Faith wanted to scream and cry and hit something.

How could this happen?

This was their miracle, their answer to a million prayers. This baby was the only thing they really wanted.

God, where are you? Why? My baby!

The doctor was saying something else, but she couldn't focus on his voice. She just wanted to go home and curl up and not think about anything ever again. Was this really happening to her?

She heard something about "letting nature take its course" or tissue and D&C. She was vaguely aware of her husband answering the doctor for both of them.

Sam. Sam was so excited about the baby. She had let him down once again. Their hands remained clasped between the chairs, as if they were a lifeline for each other on this sinking ship.

Her cheeks were wet, tears dripping off her chin. Where had those come from? She left them there. What was the point of wiping them away when more were sure to follow? She might never quit crying ever again.

More medical terms floated through the conversation. The doctor was being so matter-of-fact about the whole thing. Didn't he know she was dying right here in front of him?

This wasn't a clinical situation.

This was a tragedy.

Over and over in her head, all she could really think was, *My baby. God, why did you take my baby?*

CHAPTER 13

HOPE

*H*ope rested her head against the wall, seated sideways on her bed. Faith's sobs were muffled through the door, but she could still hear them. Saturday was supposed to be her day of rest, but there was no relaxation when sadness was trying to suffocate everyone in the house. She wanted to escape, to run and go anywhere, but that wasn't fair to her sister and brother-in-law. Driving Faith to the doctor hadn't been enough. And Sam had driven her home, which left Hope even more useless. Not that Sam hadn't expressed his appreciation for getting Faith there to begin with ... she just wished she could have done more.

What if Hope hadn't run out the week before? What if she had insisted on painting the walls and chased Faith out of the room, so she couldn't breathe in the fumes? Hope still caught a whiff of the odor even now, a week later. What if she hadn't caused that stupid quarrel that day and then stressed her sister out by disappearing all afternoon? What if Faith hadn't insisted on working at camp this week? What if? What if? What if? Would any of it have made a difference? The little bit Sam had told Hope was the baby's heart wasn't beating anymore, and Faith's body was miscarrying.

Miscarrying. No heartbeat. No more niece or nephew. Dead before she even got to meet him or her.

Hope hadn't even really told Faith how excited she was to be an aunt. She had just played it off like everything else this summer. After all, had there been anything more important to her than finding a new job in her own town? Not anything she'd let people know about. She slammed her fist on the bed and got up. The least she could do was make dinner for those who might want to eat.

Sam went through the motions of devouring his spaghetti half an hour later. He sat across the counter from her, but she could tell his mind wasn't really there. His eyes were unfocused and ringed with dark smudges from a lack of sleep, a lack of joy. Faith had claimed she wasn't hungry. Sam pushed his chair back and stood.

Before he turned to go, he placed a hand on her shoulder. "Thanks, Hope."

She just nodded.

Church services the next day were a bit awkward. The congregation seemed already to know what had happened, but most didn't know what to say. Faith had stayed home. She claimed the pain was keeping her in bed, but Hope wondered if it was physical or emotional ache. Maria came over and gave Hope and Sam big hugs, and Joe followed suit. Maysie sent home a casserole and said to call her if they needed anything else.

What they needed was for this not to have happened. But no one could undo this.

It was going to be a relief to go to camp Monday morning if only to escape the funeral feeling of the house. It wasn't that she wasn't sad to lose her niece or nephew. Her heart was broken, just as any aunt's would be. But she couldn't just sit and dwell on it, or she'd go crazy.

Hope did offer to take the week off from camp and stay with Faith, but Sam told her they'd be fine. So, she let the first-grade boys and Joe distract her from the problems at home. Yes. Camp was a big respite, with the silliness of the kids, the sunshine that reminded her that the whole world wasn't in mourning right now, the wonderful hug from Joe ...

It was silly improvisation week at camp, and she and Joe had been picked to be in charge of Sing-along after lunch on Thursday. He had an insane idea she wasn't sure they could pull off, but he said he had faith in her. He wanted them to get up and have a whole conversation, and each time one started talking, the words had to begin with the next letter of the alphabet. She thought he was crazy, but she was practicing in her head, anyway. She had come up with several ways the conversation could go with her only having to sing the alphabet song in her head twice to remember which letter came next, but she also wasn't standing in front of the whole camp as she washed the skillet in her sister's kitchen.

The quick dinner she had fixed for her and Sam would have fed several more, considering the small portions each had taken. Leftovers needed putting away, and she busied herself finding the right-sized container to store the food that Faith didn't have the appetite to eat. Sam had escaped to a church function, although he had stared for a long time down the hallway, as if he didn't want to leave his wife alone but was inadequate here, too. Hope understood that look—she was pretty sure she wore the same one most of the time anymore.

Mom arrived that evening. Hope let her in and accepted a hug before she pointed toward the bedroom where Faith had been hiding the last few days. Mom made her way down the hallway and quietly opened the door.

Hope could hear the sobs where she stood in the kitchen. It had been the main sound in the house off and on since Friday. And she seemed to be inept. She hoped her mom would be of more comfort than she had been.

Mom came back into the kitchen a few minutes later and perched on a stool. "How is she doing really?"

"I don't know." Hope shrugged and set the dish she had been

washing aside. "We didn't talk much before ... and now she hardly even comes out of the bedroom."

Mom nodded. "And you, Hope? How are you doing?"

Hope sat across from her mom and studied the top of the counter. "I'm trying to distract myself, I guess. I go to work and try to focus on the boys and doing everything that needs to be done there. Trying not to think about the fact that I could have had a niece or nephew there in five years, running around with those kids, doing crafts and singing silly songs."

"It's not something you ever plan to happen." Mom clasped her hands in front of her. "I lost three babies, two before Faith and one before you. When I had you girls, it was sort of like God gave me back what He had taken away, but I'll always wonder ... what would those children have been like? Would we have had a boy? Would they have had the same wavy blond hair you and Faith have or more brown like your Daddy's? I'll always wonder."

"Did she talk to you?" Hope asked.

"Not much. Just said she's mad at God again."

"Again?"

Mom let out a long breath. "It's hard to go through infertility treatments and hoping every month that it worked this time. It's hard to finally get pregnant only to not have it work out. To want something so badly and wonder why you can't have it, when it seems like it wouldn't be a bad thing to have. It's not like you're asking for money or a new car. You're asking God for a child. And when He continues to say, 'No,' it's easy to get frustrated and angry with Him."

All this time Hope had thought Faith had the perfect life. Instead, the more she stayed here this summer, the more she was seeing that behind all the outward perfection was a huge inner war that Faith was really good at hiding. It wasn't a trait Hope had ever mastered in her own life, as she was much better at just letting her emotions out in the open. At least then people knew what was going on with her and didn't have to wonder if she was okay or not. Although as she thought more about it, Hope realized she was hiding her worries about finding another teaching job this summer. Probably no one but God knew how much she was struggling with those fears.

∼

HOPE WAS glad to be at work again the next day. Faith was scheduled for her follow-up appointment to remove any remaining tissue so that she wouldn't get any infections. That was one task Hope was glad to leave up to her mom and Sam to help out with. She almost didn't want to go back to the house that evening, either.

"You okay?" Joe asked at lunch.

"Just thinking about Faith." Hope picked at her sandwich, tearing it into tiny pieces.

"How is she?" Joe asked.

Hope shrugged. "Mom came yesterday, and that seemed to help a little bit, but she's really depressed. I feel completely useless. All I do is make dinner and do dishes. She won't talk to me at all."

She helped one of the boys open his ketchup packet to dip his chicken nuggets.

Joe squeezed her arm. "As long as you're there for her, you're not useless. And with you making dinner, she doesn't have to worry about making sure Sam is fed. That's probably more of a relief than she can express. Just keep letting her know she's loved. That's what she needs right now."

Hope sighed. "It just doesn't feel like enough."

"You can't do everything, Hope." Joe popped the top on a soda for another boy. He pointed at the boy as he sat down. "You need to drink that pretty fast or you're not going to have time to finish it before Sing-along."

"I'm still not sure that us doing Sing-along in a couple days is a good idea. I really don't think I can do this." Hope dusted her crumbs behind the cubby, where the ants and birds could enjoy them.

"Sure you can." Joe handed her a candy bar from his own lunch box. "We can practice a couple of times between now and then, and it will be perfect."

"When will we practice? We're watching these guys every moment of every day." Hope motioned to the sixteen first-graders sitting around them.

Joe made a thoughtful face. "Hmm. Guess we might have to get together outside of work hours."

"Oh really?" Hope couldn't stop her grin. "And when would we do that?"

"I'm free tonight." Joe gave a shrug that was more nonchalant than he was coming across.

"Start cleaning up, boys." Hope raised her voice to be heard by the whole cubby. "That was the bell to go to Sing-along."

"You didn't answer my question." Joe stood up.

"What question would that be? I didn't hear a question." Hope popped the last bite of chocolate into her mouth.

Joe grinned as he walked out to the trash can. Hope helped several boys zip up lunch boxes and pick up a few pieces of litter. Joe lifted their basket onto his hip.

"Line up behind Ms. Hope and follow her to Sing-along, boys." Joe pointed to her before he carried their things back to the main building.

The third-grade counselors had Sing-along today, and their improvisation skit was different than Joe's idea. They had asked some other counselors to come up with several props, and then they had to decide what those objects could be used for other than what they were really meant for. Someone handed them a pool noodle. One of them pretended it was a horse. Another used it as a scarf. Then, the first one decided it was a horn. The kids were laughing like crazy as they watched.

"So, pick you up around six tonight?" Joe appeared beside Hope on the sidelines.

Hope considered her alternative—staying at Faith's house, where happiness didn't seem to be allowed right now, or hanging out with this great teddy bear of a guy who continually had her grinning.

"Okay." Hope said.

CHAPTER 14

FAITH

"I talked to your daddy earlier today. He's wishing he was here, too." Mom perched on the edge of Faith's bed. They had been home from the doctor for around an hour, and she was checking on Faith.

"I know he had to work. And he doesn't need to come." Faith picked at a loose thread on the blanket. "You didn't really have to come all this way, Mom."

"Of course, I did. There was no way I was going to let you go through this alone."

"I'm not alone. Sam's here." Faith pointed toward the doorway. "And Hope."

"But sometimes it's nice to have your mom."

Faith ducked her head. "Yes. Sometimes it's nice to have your mom."

"Do you need anything?" Mom gave her hand a squeeze.

"For none of this to have happened." She felt the tears start to well up once again. Would she ever be able to go more than a few minutes without crying?

"I wish I could snap my fingers and make that the case, Sweetie."

"I know you can't. No one can make this better." Faith shook her head.

"You're always going to miss this baby. I won't tell you otherwise." Mom leaned forward until she was in Faith's line of sight. "But you can go on from here and still have a good life. This isn't the end of your story. And God will help you through—if you'll let Him."

"It feels like God is very far away right now." Faith fisted the covers in her hand. "Why bother letting me get pregnant in the first place if He was just going to take the baby away again?"

"God's not the one who took your baby away."

"But He didn't keep it from happening, either." Faith couldn't keep the anger out of her voice. "One week, we were perfectly fine and healthy and everything looked great. Two weeks later, we're here. Why? What's the point of all this?"

"You'll probably never know why." Mom cupped her cheek gently with her hand. "But none of this changes who God is. Or that He loves you. He's still there, still listening and waiting and wanting to help you through this. As we all are. As you pointed out, you're not alone."

"If this is love, I'm not sure I want it." Faith turned her face away.

"It took me a long time to get through it, too, when I lost my first baby." Mom leaned back. "I sounded a lot like you, trying to figure out what I had done wrong, what I could have done differently, why that baby had to die so young."

"How did you get past it? Was it when you got pregnant with me?" Faith rested her hand on her empty belly.

"No." Mom shook her head. "You were and are a huge blessing in my life, but you're not what brought me back to a good relationship with God. I had a good friend back then who came and visited me several days a week. I was in a really bad place, trying to blame God for everything, not sure of the purpose of my life or how to get past it. My friend Cathy came over and was listening to me say much the same as what you were saying. And then she reminded me of something. Just because bad things had happened in my life, it didn't mean God was bad. God was the same. He never changes. I just had to agree to see that in my life instead of only focusing on what was wrong."

"I'm not sure how to do that." Faith nibbled her bottom lip for a moment. "I'm not sure how to get past the sadness and hurt."

"It's still really fresh. Your wounds are raw." Mom patted her knee. "But hang in there. Take it one day at a time. Let yourself grieve. Let yourself heal. Let the people around you help. And don't neglect God just because you feel like He's neglected you. He hasn't. You just can't see it right now."

Faith swiped at the wetness on her cheeks.

"I hate that I have to go back so soon." Mom stood up. "I don't want to leave you like this."

"I'll be okay. I know you need to get back to Dad."

Mom laughed. "Yeah. He couldn't find his black socks earlier. That man. I love him, but I think when he went into partial retirement, he put his brain there, too."

Faith felt a small grin creep up the edges of her mouth.

"Call if you need anything." Mom kissed her forehead like she was a child again. "I'm not leaving until tomorrow."

∽

FAITH SAT in the bathtub that evening, the hot shower running over her head. She could still hear the sounds of the machine as it ripped what was left of her precious child from her womb. *Tissue.* That's what the doctor had called what they were removing. *Tissue.* He acted like it hadn't been a life, even though he had heard the heartbeat just as clearly as she had two weeks before.

Deep down inside, she knew that it had to be done to keep her healthy. She just felt so dirty to have had a process used on her that was typically used in abortions. Normally, it was one of the ways women eliminated unwanted babies, but she had desired hers so much.

"It's not fair." She sobbed, her forehead resting on her knees. "God, it's not fair."

The water dripped off her hair and mixed with her hot tears until she couldn't tell how much of the moisture on her face was from emotion and how much was from the shower. Maybe both were cleansing. Considering how much she had cried over the last four days, it still surprised her that she had any tears left at all.

She covered her flat abdomen with her hand and wished for the tiny bump that had been starting to appear. It was gone—all trace and evidence of her recent pregnancy was gone, as if it had never happened. The three pairs of maternity pants she bought two weeks ago would sit unworn in her dresser, a waste of money and dreams.

But it *had* happened. She had a picture somewhere of the pregnancy test that had finally shown two little blue lines instead of one. She had been having Sam take pictures and help measure her belly every week to document the growth—even though there hadn't been much up to that point, there had been *some*. She had the doctor bills from her first ultrasound just a few weeks before, when everything was still looking great and perfect.

"Why, God? Why did you let this happen?"

She had opened a card from a well-meaning friend today that said, "Thinking of you in this hard time. Even though this is so very hard on you, we're all glad to know you can get pregnant, something we thought you couldn't do for a while." The friend had finished it off by writing out Romans 8:28. "And we know that all things work together for good to those who love God, to those who are the called according to His purpose."

"How could someone think that was comforting?" Hope had exclaimed when she saw it. "That's horrible!"

Mom had taken Hope aside and explained that not everyone realized that losing a baby at ten weeks of pregnancy hurt just as badly as losing one after it was born. Hope had shaken her head and looked at Faith with sorrow in her eyes. It was a look Faith hadn't expected to see from her sister after all the fighting they had done over the last few years. Even though she had thought they might be making progress in their relationship these past weeks, things still seemed at odds with them most of the time. She wasn't sure what to do with her sister's sympathy.

She studied her wrinkled fingers and wondered how much longer the hot water would hold out. She had to have been in here for almost an hour. She thought about standing up and getting out, but she didn't have the energy. The door to the bathroom squeaked open, and she frowned.

Sam leaned through the curtain and turned off the faucet. He grabbed a towel and wrapped it around her and lifted her out of the tub. She stood there while he dried her off, carefully patting the towel over her body. Didn't he find her completely repulsive? He slipped her nightgown over her head and let his hands follow it down the contours of her body. He kissed her forehead and her cheeks where tears still made slow tracks. He kissed her nose and her chin. Then, her lips.

She looked up at him. "I'm sorry."

"For what?" He brushed her wet hair out of her face.

"For not being able to give you a child, to make you a Daddy. For letting you down again."

"You have never let me down." He clasped her face in his hands so that she had to meet his eyes. "Never. And this is not your fault, Faith."

"It *is* my fault. I can't even do the one thing a woman is supposed to be able to do. I can't reproduce. It can't be that hard!" Faith threw her arms up in exasperation. "It seems like every time you look at the tabloids, another movie star is pregnant or another teenager. All of them unmarried. Why is it that we did everything right and still can't have the one thing we want the most in the world?"

Sam pulled her to his chest and held her tight. His heartbeat thrummed against her cheek. She snuggled further into him and cried for another minute.

Finally, she leaned back enough to look at him. "Do you ever wonder what would have happened if you had married someone else? Maybe you could have kids by now and—"

Sam put his fingers over her mouth. "I didn't want to marry anyone else. I wanted to marry you. And I didn't marry you for your reproductive organs, either. I married you because I love you."

"But now you're cursed with such a horrible wife."

"I'm not cursed with a horrible wife." He shook his head. "I'm blessed with you."

"What if we can't ever have a child?" Faith whispered.

"Then, we'll have more time to travel."

She tried to fight it, but a smile tilted up the corner of her mouth. "Sam McCreary stop it! I'm trying to be serious here, and you don't mean that."

"We'll cross that bridge if and when we have to." Sam pressed his forehead to hers. "But we're not there yet, Faith. Your mom was able to have you after she miscarried. It's still a possibility for us. Just not right now."

"How can I get through this? How can I find the strength to go forward and even think about possibilities like that? There's no closure here. We can't even have a funeral. There's no ... there's no body to bury." She covered her tummy with her hand again. "It's like they have erased every evidence of it ever happening."

"God has our child in His hands. He's taking care of it now. Just think about how great it is that our child isn't ever going to have to feel pain or be sad or have to suffer at all." Sam leaned back against the sink. "That doesn't mean we won't miss it. It just means that once we get past the worst of the ache, maybe we can find the peace that comes with the knowledge of our God's love. That's what I'm holding on to."

"We didn't even know if it was a boy or a girl." A sob caught in the back of her throat.

"It was a girl." Sam chucked her under her chin. "You told me it was."

"Can we give her a name even though she was never really born?" Faith whispered.

"What name would you give her?" Sam asked, emotion thick in his voice. "I know we had talked about a few name possibilities, but we hadn't really decided on one for sure."

Faith smiled through her tears. "My sister and I used to love the name Moira Angela when we were little. We had this doll that we loved, and we named her that. We would fight over who got to be Moira Angela and who had to be one of the other dolls when we played together. Let's name her Moira Angela McCreary."

"What if you wanted to use that name later?" Sam asked.

"I don't think she'd mind sharing it."

He kissed her forehead again. "Come on, Beautiful. It's been a long day. To bed with you."

It was still early, barely even nine, but she could see the weariness in her husband's face. *He's hurting, too.* The realization took her breath away. *I've been so wrapped up in myself, relying on him, when he's hurting just like me.* It was like a sucker punch. Whom else had she been neglecting the last few days? Where was Hope? She'd worry about her sister later. Right now, she needed to show her husband some of the support he had been selflessly dishing out for her. She lay down beside him and ran her fingers through his hair until he drifted off.

Faith got back up after Sam had fallen asleep. She didn't want to wake him with her tossing and turning. She pulled a robe around her and padded to the kitchen for a cup of milk. In the living room in the dark, she sat and listened to the creak of the house settling, the cars going by, the cicadas humming so loudly she could hear them through the walls.

"I'm still not happy with you, God," she whispered.

CHAPTER 15

HOPE

"So, I asked Steve to get a couple of the kids to volunteer to come up with some scenes for us to act out when we do this on Thursday." Joe had polished off half the pizza between them in the time it had taken Hope to eat most of two slices.

"So, in other words, we really have no idea what we're going to end up doing, even if we are practicing tonight?"

"Right." Joe picked a piece of pepperoni off the remaining pie and ate it. "But since that's the meaning of improvisation, I guess that makes sense."

"Who came up with this theme? Why couldn't we have ended up 'volunteering' for 'dancing with the counselors' week?" Hope propped her chin on her fist.

"Well, if you still want to volunteer for that, they are looking for a few more counselors." Joe cocked an eyebrow.

"No. Can't dance. No rhythm." Hope threw her hands in the air. "Guess I'm stuck with this one. So how do we practice for something we don't know?"

Joe paused for a moment, and she could almost see the wheels turning in his head. "Well, we can just toss out a few scenarios of our own and see what we can come up with."

"O-kaaay." Hope stretched out the word to show her skepticism. "What's a scenario the kids might come up with?"

"Depends on the age of the kid."

She nodded in agreement. "What about dinosaurs are chasing us?"

He looked impressed. "Okay. First one of us to miss starting with the next letter of the alphabet loses that round. Ready?"

She shook her head.

"Too bad. Next words out of our mouths have to be in alphabetical order." Joe rolled the die he had borrowed from a word game at home. The oddly shaped polyhedron stopped with the letter *I* facing up.

She thought for a moment before she said, "I … don't know what to do."

He widened his eyes and then guffawed. "I got nothing."

She laughed. "So, I guess we better hope they don't suggest that scene."

"Hm. Okay. What about a day at the pool?" He leaned back in his seat. "They might say something like that since we're at camp."

Another roll of the die. This time they were to start with *S*.

"Splish, splash."

"Throw me the beach ball!" He grinned.

She thought a second to remember what letter came next. "Ugh! I got water in my ears."

"Very nice swimsuit."

"Water, water everywhere."

He looked at her for a minute as if he couldn't think of anything and then he got a gleam in his eye. "X-ray tetras do not belong on the pool! Keep your fish out of there."

Shoot! She had been sure he'd trip over *X*. Okay. Two could play the game of scolding. "You better not run!"

He wiggled his eyebrows. "Zoos are for animals. Quit monkeying around."

"Are you kidding me?"

"Booyah! That is how you play this game!" He pointed to her with a grin.

"That doesn't count!" She shook her head.

"Sure, it does. It does if *ugh* does. It's not like we're honestly going to say that at the swimming pool tomorrow." His smug look said he thought he won.

"*Booyah* shouldn't count. It's not a real word." She crossed her arms.

He held his hands up in defeat. "Truce. Let's do something maybe an older kid would suggest ... what about boyfriend and girlfriend having an argument?"

The die landed on *D*.

She thought for a moment. "Don't break my heart."

"Eventually this had to happen."

"First time for everything?"

"Great relationships are never easy." He shrugged.

She laughed before answering back. "Haters never win, though."

"I love you." He gave a great dramatic performance of clasping his hands over his heart and fluttering his eyelashes.

Her heart skipped a beat. His actions said he was just playing the game, but those words ... they had sounded real. What was the next letter after *I*?

She threw her hands up in defeat. "How can I come up with a reply to that?"

He paid the waitress and loaded their leftover pizza into a to-go box. They walked out into the evening air, only slightly cooler now than it had been earlier in the day. She climbed up in his old Jeep and buckled herself in.

"I really think our biggest hurdle is just building your confidence up." Joe carefully pulled out into traffic.

"Hey!"

"Hope, you're really smart, but sometimes it's like you don't believe in yourself or in anything. Like you're just going through the motions of whatever is before you and not holding out for anything better."

Hope studied him with her mouth slightly open. "Why would you say that?"

"You're still bummed out about your car being wrecked over a month ago, even though you already have a better one to drive. You don't have a job lined up for this fall, but when you get an offer to find one, you turn it down because it wasn't what you considered to be perfect, even though it's teaching. You hate that you're living at Faith's house, even though you're not having to pay rent and you're being well-fed. You have a fun job this summer, but you still don't enjoy it because you think you're not very good at it." He ticked each reason off on his fingers as if he had made this list before he picked her up this evening.

"Says the man whose life is just perfect. Because you're working at your favorite camp in the state you love and you're off to do your mission work at the end of the summer, which is your dream job … But you still haven't told Maria you're going. So, maybe your life isn't as perfect as you think."

He glanced at her out of the corner of his eye before changing lanes. "I'm not trying to criticize. I'm just saying you don't give yourself enough credit. You have a lot going for you, but it's like you refuse to see the silver lining in anything. I saw the way you were looking the other night in class when we were studying James. You put this mask over your face like you don't want to admit that maybe God's right and the trials can make us be the Christians we're supposed to be. You're too busy focusing on the trials and not the outcome."

"And what good outcome could possibly come from all of the stuff you listed that I'm apparently caught up on?" Hope knew she was on the defensive, but she couldn't help herself. Even if he was right—and he might be a *little bit* right—that didn't mean he should say all of this.

"Well, you got to meet me." Joe gave a half-grin. "So, it can't be all bad, right?"

He was possibly the best thing to come out of all of this, but she wasn't about to admit that to him, especially after everything he had just said.

"You're saying that you'll just make up for all of the bad stuff in my life?" She gave him a no-nonsense "yeah right" look.

"No." He held up a hand in defense. "No, *Chica*. God's the only one who can fill in the gaps in your life. But you're not letting Him."

"How did we even get off on all of this? We were having so much fun at dinner, and then suddenly you lambast me with all of this. What's going on?"

He sighed. "I'm just worried about you. You're my friend now, and I see the way you're taking everything so hard. I want to help, but it's like you're putting up this wall between us and not letting me in. You give me little answers when I ask what's going on, but you don't want to talk about the whole story. I just wanted to see if I could help."

She recognized some of the houses they were passing and knew he was almost back to Faith and Sam's. "So, you decided to attack me at the end of a perfect evening."

"I didn't mean for it to come across as an attack. I just wanted to make sure you saw how good you were when we practiced earlier and make sure you knew I thought you were doing great as a counselor, too." Joe parked in the driveway.

"I'm not a good counselor. Mostly I just help you."

"The boys love you. They're always showing you tricks in the swimming pool, and they'd much rather have you help them with crafts than me. You're great at doing little things like drawing smiley faces with the ketchup or adding details to the sand castle. And you're perfect when you cheer them on during kickball—not to mention that they think your new scars are really neat." He ran a finger lightly over the shoulder she had scraped on counselor night.

She looked down and then over at him. Why was it that every

time he touched her, her pulse sped up just a bit more? "They're just scars."

"But the fact that you did a flip when you fell after your amazing one-base kick and then wiping out not only your shoulder, but your knee, too. Man! That's what first-grade boys think is really cool." Joe punched his fist in the air. His voice got a little softer as he glanced back her direction. "And sometimes twenty-six-year-old boys think so, too."

Her heart caught in her throat. His deep brown eyes studied hers in the glow from the streetlight. He leaned closer, paused. She swayed his direction, lost in his look, in the moment, forgetting all the strife of a few minutes before. He must have taken it as permission because he touched his lips to hers. Then, he leaned in a little farther and deepened the kiss, his hand coming up and cradling her cheek. She clasped his arm, gave in to the amazing, heady moment ... until her brain caught up with the rest of her.

She pulled back and gasped. "Joe, what are we doing?"

He frowned a bit. "Kissing?"

She backed up to her door to put more space between them. "You're possibly going to Honduras in a few months. I'll go back to Mississippi. Where does that leave us? Where does that leave this?"

"I'm sorry. I guess I wasn't thinking about the end of the summer yet. I thought what I read in your eyes said you wanted me to kiss you now." Joe sat back in his seat.

"No." Hope ran a hand through her hair. "I mean, I did—" She ignored the triumphant smirk that crossed his face. "But I just don't see how it's going to work. How is getting into a relationship like this any better than the one I just ended?"

"I didn't realize you just ended a relationship."

Was that jealousy in his voice?

"I was dating a guy back home for several years until I realized the relationship wasn't going anywhere." She shook her head. "And this one has nowhere to go, either. I'm sorry, Joe." She got out of the car before she could say anything else.

She heard him getting out of the Jeep, too, so Hope hurried to the door to let herself in. His hand covered hers as she turned the key. She looked up into his eyes. He was so close, only a breath away. Why was she running away again? Was he right? Could they just enjoy the moment? She fought the temptation to close the gap and continue where they had left off in the car. With every ounce of self-will she had, she pulled back just a bit farther, where she couldn't smell his cologne or see the shadow of stubble along his jawline.

"I'm sorry, Hope. Please don't be mad at me." His voice was soft and earnest.

"I'm not mad at you, Joe." She turned the handle. "I'm mad at the whole situation." And she slipped in the door before he could stop her again.

CHAPTER 16

FAITH

Faith looked up from her computer screen as Hope rushed through the front door. "Was that Joe?"

That answered her earlier pondering about where her sister was. Those two had been spending an awful lot of time together.

Hope hastily swiped her hands on her face and nodded. "Sorry. I didn't know you were sitting there."

"Hope, what's wrong?" Faith set her laptop aside. Updating her blog could wait. She still wasn't sure exactly what to write anyway.

Hope took a shaky breath. "He kissed me."

"And you didn't want him to?" Faith couldn't understand why that would make her sister cry. Faith had secretly been harboring a hope that the two of them would get together so she could have Joe in her family officially.

"No. I did want him to." Hope pressed her hand to her forehead as if to clear her mind. "But he shouldn't have."

Faith stood slowly and walked to Hope. "You're not making any sense." She steered her sister over to the couch and pulled her down.

"Joe's talking about moving to Honduras in the fall. He wants to join a missionary team already down there that's losing one of their members. He's even got most of his sponsors lined up. But don't tell

Maria. He hasn't figured out how to tell her yet." Hope collapsed back into the cushions.

"Honduras?" Where on earth had that come from? Her Joe was moving away ... to another country? But it did make sense, if she thought about it. Joe was one of the most mission-minded people she knew. Poor Maria.

"Yeah. So now you can see why he shouldn't kiss me." Hope flopped her hands in her lap. "There's nowhere for our relationship to go. I don't even know what I'm going to be doing this fall, but it's not going to be anywhere close to Honduras. I mean, I don't know what to do. I like Joe, but I feel like I'm just going to get my heart broken if I let myself fall for him."

Faith hugged her sister. "That's tough. I have no idea what to tell you. I think Joe's great. You know that. But you have to do what's best for you, too."

Hope laid her head in Faith's lap, like she had done when they were in middle and high school, on the rare occasions they had gotten along and talked. The initial time must have been when Hope had broken up with her first real boyfriend. Hope had been in eighth grade. His name was Tommy Miles. She had dumped him because he couldn't keep his eyes off another girl in their class and she didn't trust him—but her heart was shattered.

Faith had held her like this, running her fingers through her hair and telling her there were other fish in the sea. This time, though, she wasn't sure that was the case. Joe was about as good a catch as you could get.

Oh, Joe. This wasn't the way this was supposed to play out. What are you doing, Friend?

"How long will he be in Honduras?" Faith asked.

"I don't know." Hope choked on a sob. "But I don't want to wait forever to get married. I already feel like I'm an old maid."

"You're twenty-four. You're not an old maid."

"But I *feel* like one. Most of my friends from college are already married. Some of them even have kids. I feel like I'm getting left behind. And now I don't even have my job. At least up till April I had my dream job. Now, what do I have?"

Faith gently trailed her fingers along the sides of Hope's head and down through her ponytail. "I know how it feels when you think all your friends are moving on to the next part of their lives without you, but you'll survive."

"Thanks a lot." Hope's voice was full of sarcasm.

Okay, so maybe telling her she would survive wasn't the most comforting thing to say. She wouldn't want anyone telling her that, either. Change of tactic.

"Who's to say Joe's not the right guy for you? If he kissed you, he must be pretty smitten. Joe's not the kind of guy to just go kissing any girl."

"I know that." Hope wiped a remaining tear away. "But it doesn't mean we won't have to be apart again at the end of the summer. It's almost July already. I've only got another month or so before I have to have a job and figure out exactly what I'm doing with my life."

Faith reigned in her desire to shake her head. Her sister had always been one for dramatics. "You make it sound like it's going to be a life or death thing if you don't find a teaching job this school year. What if you take a year off and figure out exactly what you want to do?"

"How would I live? I don't have enough in savings to do that, especially with a new car." Hope punched the sofa cushion next to her.

"Mom was saying she wouldn't mind having you home again for a year."

Hope groaned out loud. Yeah. Faith admitted moving back in with their parents, as much as they loved them, would not be a top choice for her, either.

"Or there's other things teachers could do. You could work at one of those tutoring places or work in a university. I know you love Ole Miss. Why not see if a professor there needs help?" Faith squeezed Hope's shoulder.

Hope was quiet for a moment. "Or check out the teacher's job fair here that you wanted me to go to."

Faith leaned over to look at her sister's face. "But you hate it here."

"It's been pointed out to me several times that maybe I'm looking a gift horse in the mouth and being ungrateful." Hope made a face to go with her sardonic reply.

Faith laughed. "I didn't say it."

"Joe did. Not in those words exactly, but that's the summation."

"And you let him kiss you anyway?" Faith raised an eyebrow.

"He also said some really nice things about me." Hope rolled over and met Faith's eyes. "I don't know. It's like, when I'm around him even the things that annoy me don't really annoy me that much. He's got this way of making sure everything is balanced just right, the good with the bad. And he just ... he makes me feel ... I can't even explain it. But evidently when he told me he thought it was really cool that I flipped the other night at camp when I fell playing kickball, I lost whatever brain power I had."

"That Joe. He's fun and handsome and sincere." Faith grinned. "And he's a pretty smart guy."

"Yeah." Hope sighed. "I know."

The way Hope was talking about Joe reminded Faith of how she had been when she and Sam first got together. It made her regret even more how she had neglected him the last few days. She mentally noted to herself to pay more attention to others. Being here for Hope right now was a good start.

"Wait. Why did you go out with him if you knew the relationship couldn't go anywhere?" Faith asked.

"We were supposed to be practicing for the thing we're doing in Sing-along on Thursday, but it changed subjects when we left the pizza place." Hope blew a stray hair off her face.

"What week is it? I can't even remember the theme." Faith frowned. "I've sort of been in my own little world."

"Improvisation Week." Hope sat up and looked at Faith. "I didn't even ask how you're doing."

"That's okay." Faith ducked her head, kept herself from touching her empty belly. Just that slight reminder had been enough to send a fresh stab through her heart, but she was tired of crying. "I'd rather focus on your problems than my own. They seem easier to solve."

Hope rolled her eyes. "They wouldn't seem that way if you were me."

"Probably not." Faith gave half a smile.

The sisters sat in the dark for a while, each lost in their own thoughts.

"Remember that doll we used to have?" Faith broke the silence. "The one we always wanted to play with more than the others?"

"Moira Angela?" Hope asked.

"Yes." Faith smiled. "I was talking to Sam earlier about the baby. We didn't even know if it was a girl or a boy."

She paused to regain control of herself. Blast these tears! How could she even have any tears left, as many as she had already shed the last few days? She took a deep breath so she could share the rest of the story.

"He said it must have been a girl because I was so sure it was. So, we decided to call her Moira. I know he wouldn't really want to name a daughter that, but since this one ..."

Hope reached out and caught Faith's hand. "It's a great idea."

"I knew you'd understand."

Faith stayed on the couch a bit longer after Hope had headed to bed. Having been in bed so much the last few days, it was nice to sit on something else for a while. And with her mind going a million miles a minute still, she was afraid she would bother Sam if she returned to their room just yet.

Mom was headed back to Tennessee in the morning. As much as she appreciated her mother being there the last few days, it would be nice to get back to normal ... whatever that might mean. Would things go back to exactly the way they were before Moira came into their life? She shook her head.

No. Even after only a few months of knowing they would be parents their lives were changed completely. And not just the color of the walls in the spare room.

So, she would take it one day at a time. And slowly, she would figure out what normal was now.

CHAPTER 17

HOPE

Hope wasn't sure what to expect when she saw Joe the next morning, but he acted like nothing was different between the two of them. He greeted everyone with his normal huge smile. He went about the morning routine like he had never even thought about kissing Hope, and especially not the night before. Hope was almost hurt that it didn't seem like anything had changed between the two of them, but she was more relieved.

It was only slightly different that night at Bible study. He didn't give her any particular looks when she got to class. Instead, he almost avoided her.

"We're still in James chapter one tonight." He opened his Bible and leaned casually against the podium. "Last week we talked about temptation and how it doesn't come from God. It comes from our own desires. This week let's start at verse 16."

"'Do not be deceived, my beloved brethren. Every good gift and every perfect gift is from above, and comes down from the Father of lights, with whom there is no variation or shadow of turning. Of His own will He brought us forth by the word of truth, that we might be a kind of firstfruits of His creatures.'"

"When you think of God, you need to think 'God *equals* good.'

Like in a math equation. Because that's what He is, and therefore, nothing bad can come from Him, like we talked about last week when we were talking about how temptations don't come from Him. Isn't it great that we serve a God like that?" Joe asked.

"Yes!" A redhead in the back spoke up. "Just yesterday I was thinking about everything that has happened in the last four years since I became a Christian. And I can literally see God blessing me. Before I started coming to church and studying, I never would have believed how much better my life could be."

"It's like when we give more to God and He gives us more in return." A guy right behind Hope waved his Bible around as he spoke. "It doesn't seem like you'd end up with more when you're giving more away, but it always works out that way."

Hope wanted to turn around and tell him he was an idiot and that it didn't always work out that way, but she decided she better not stir things up quite that much, especially since she was only a visitor here.

"We just have to remember to thank God every time we recognize the good things He's doing in our life." Another guy in the front of the class leaned forward as he talked. "A lot of times we forget, and I wonder what we would do if God ever quit giving us the things we never thank Him for."

Another typical Bible school answer. Hope was getting tired of typical Bible school answers.

"What about the bad stuff?" Hope almost stopped there when everyone turned to look at her, but she was riled up enough that she pushed ahead. "If God doesn't want it to happen, why does it? Why do people lose babies after they've been trying to have them for four years? Why do people lose jobs or ... get cancer or whatever? We're all Christians, and we follow God. But bad stuff keeps happening. Isn't He supposed to be giving us good stuff?"

Joe raised an eyebrow as he made full eye contact with her for the first time that evening. "Just because it isn't good doesn't mean it can't happen. We live in a sinful world. We're surrounded by people who don't follow God. Sometimes, their bad stuff affects our lives just like sometimes our good stuff affects theirs. But just because something bad happens doesn't mean something good can't come of it. That's what we were talking about several weeks ago when we were talking about verse two.

"'Count it all joy when you fall into various trials.' It doesn't mean you're going to be happy something bad happened. But you can be glad to know you can grow from it and become a better person because that bad thing affected your life."

Hope hated it that he was right. She knew he was even as she listened to him say it, but that didn't mean she wanted to accept it. It was like she couldn't let go of her anger toward life and how it had treated her earlier this year. And how it was now abusing her sister. Sure, they might not always get along, but they were still siblings.

"Are you really struggling with that as much as you seem to be?" Joe caught up to her after class as she walked down the hall.

"Talking to me again, are you?" She hugged her Bible to her chest.

"Hope, I'm sorry. I didn't know how to deal with it, I guess. With everything that happened last night ..."

"I know." She studied the faded tiles on the floor.

"How can I help you with your struggles?" He put his hand on her arm. "Hope?"

She finally looked back up at him. "I don't know. I guess sometimes I can't see the point of being a Christian if we're going to have to suffer just as much as everyone else. What's the point?"

"Really? You really can't see why it's better to be a Christian?" He looked so concerned.

"I mean, yes, Heaven and all of that, but what about here? Do we really have to wait to get to Heaven before things can be good?" Hope didn't even know where this was coming from. When had she started thinking these things? Sure, she had been upset with God over how life had gone lately, but she hadn't realized just how much she was holding against Him.

"Is your life really so bad, Hope?" Joe squeezed her fingers.

"There you are." Maria joined them from the other direction.

Hope suddenly realized Joe had grabbed her hand, and she pulled away quickly. She took a quick breath to try and calm her heart before turning to her sweet friend. "Hey, Maria."

"You two look so good together." Maria wiggled her eyebrows.

Joe and Hope exchanged uncomfortable glances.

"What? Did I interrupt something?" Maria pointed between the two of them.

"No, Mama." Joe shook his head. "I was just about to invite Hope over for dinner tomorrow night. You know, to celebrate how great we're going to do at Sing-along."

Hope cocked an eyebrow.

He gave her a look that screamed, "Please."

"I'll have to make sure Faith doesn't have any plans." Hope shrugged. She wasn't sure what was going on with Joe, but he was acting very twitchy.

"Have to check with Faith about what?" Faith appeared beside Hope. It was Faith's first time back to a church service since losing the baby—she had figured a Wednesday night Bible study might be easier than a Sunday morning.

"It's so good to see you out and about again, dear." Maria wrapped Faith up in a big hug and held on tight for a full minute. "We're praying."

Faith pulled away and gave a half-smile. "Thanks. So, what was Hope needing to check with me about?"

"Evidently, we're inviting Hope over for dinner tomorrow night." Maria grinned. "Did you have plans? Maybe you and Sam could join us, too."

Joe's eyes grew a little wider at that before he controlled his facial expression again. "Sure. That would be great."

"I actually decided to go ahead and keep my card-making meeting tomorrow evening. I figured it would be good to get together with my ladies again. Maybe next time." Faith smirked at Joe.

Hope frowned at him. What was going on? He refused to meet her glance though, until right before the group broke up to go their separate ways for the evening.

He leaned close to her and whispered, "I need some support while I tell my mama I'm leaving this fall."

Her heart took an elevator straight to her feet. He just needed her as a buffer.

"Oh." She wasn't sure how she could say even that much when it felt like all the air had left her lungs.

"I finally got the rest of the details worked out. Besides, someone told me yesterday that I should have told her before now."

Hope chewed on her bottom lip to keep it from quivering and then offered a shaky smile. "Sure, Joe. I'll come."

"Thanks. See you in the morning."

"We'll talk alphabetically." She nodded. In her head, she thought about what Joe had asked right before his mom walked up. Was her life really so bad? With Joe out of the picture … yes. A resounding *yes*.

∼

AS HOPE STOOD NERVOUSLY on the small platform in front of everyone at camp, she wondered again how she had let Joe talk her into this. Surely there had to be a better option for entertaining kids. Instead, here she was, her fingers trying not to shake as they clutched the microphone.

"Here are the rules." Steve held his hands up to get everyone's attention. "Joe and Hope have to take turns talking, which isn't too hard. But today, each time they start to talk, they have to start with the next letter of the alphabet. So, if Joe says something that starts with a *J*, Hope will have to reply with something that starts with a *K*. And they only have seven seconds to start talking with the next letter or they forfeit and the other one wins. We're going to do rock, paper, scissors to see which one of them has to start first. Ready, you two?"

Hope and Joe nodded as they clutched their fist in front of each other. "One, two, three. Rock, paper, scissors!"

Joe held a fist. Hope's hand was flat. She won. She would start them off. She wasn't sure if that was really good or really bad.

Steve held the microphone out to one of the first-grade boys and asked him what Joe and Hope should act out. "Going to the circus."

Another boy got to pick the letter to start them off. "*H* for *Hope*!"

Hope panicked for a moment. What started with an *H* that had anything to do with a circus? "Hey look! The flying trapeze." Her voice shook a bit, but once she got going, it sounded okay.

The boys cheered her on.

Now, it was Joe's turn. "I think I see some clowns."

Hope nodded and then grinned. "Just look at that elephant!"

Joe gave her a two-can-play-this-game look. "Lions! Look at the lions."

"Uh oh!" Steve broke in. "What letter was supposed to come after *J*?"

"*K*!" From the volume of the campers' voices, it was evident even the pre-kindergartners knew their alphabet.

"I think Mr. Joe skipped ahead, don't you?" Steve held up Hope's hand as she contained a giggle of mirth at being the first winner.

Joe looked like he might protest that one, but then he gave a nod. Unfortunately for him, he couldn't deny the truth. Hope raised her arms in triumph. She had won the first round. The first-grade boys and fourth grade girls cheered the loudest.

"What do you think, guys?" Steve asked. "Should we give Mr. Joe another chance?"

"Yeah!"

"Okay, let's get a girl to give us an idea this time." He held the microphone out to one of the older girls. Hope waited to see what would come out.

"Shopping trip."

"Joe, since you lost the last round, you get to start this one." Steve pointed at him.

The letter picked this time was *M*.

Joe grinned and then pretended to hold up an article of clothing. "Muscle shirts just make me look so hot."

Although she secretly admitted his last statement was true, Hope had to remember to not just agree with him. This was a competition. She shook her finger his direction. "Needs more sleeves."

"Oh really? What about your outfit?"

"Pumps would look nice with it, right?" Hope strutted across the stage.

Joe grinned as if he didn't have one of the hardest letters in the alphabet next. "Quit showing off, and let's go check out."

Several of the counselors laughed loudly at that one.

"Right after I go look at the clearance racks." Hope hooked her thumb behind her.

Joe shook his head. "Stop spending all my money."

Hope tried to think of what she could say next. *T* was one of the easiest letters to start a word with in normal circumstances. She couldn't let Joe win after she had pulled off the first round so well. Her mind was absolutely blank.

"Time!"

Joe threw his hands up in the air and did a little victory dance.

"Let's hear it for Mr. Joe and Ms. Hope. Aren't the first-grade boys lucky to have such great counselors?" Steve asked as the kids cheered.

Joe and Hope shook hands with a grin. He might have held on to her hand just a tad longer than was necessary, but she didn't mind. They had done it. It had been a complete success. Now, to get through the rest of the day ... and the evening at Maria's.

∾

Hope still wasn't sure how she was going to be a support in this conversation, but she sat across from Maria and beside Joe later that evening, finishing off her last bite of sopapilla cheesecake. Tex-Mex was definitely one thing she did like about Texas. She took a sip of coffee and listened to Maria gush again about how well she and Joe had done at Sing-along that afternoon.

"I know Joe said you guys had practiced, but it was just perfect." Maria waved her hands in the air as she talked. "I think the kids enjoyed it, too."

"It may be a new hit." Joe leaned back.

"You could do it again next year." Maria smiled across at her son, and Hope could see the pride shining in her eyes.

"Well ..." Joe scooted back from the table a bit. "I can't."

Maria gave a small frown. "Steve didn't like it?"

"No, Steve thought it was great." Joe picked at a crumb on the tablecloth in front of him. "You know how Steve is. He's all for more ideas for theme weeks."

"So, why can't you do it again next year?"

Hope controlled the urge to reach over and grab Joe's restless arms. She couldn't save him from this. He was going to have to tell his mother his plans, and he needed to do it soon so he could start getting ready to move after summer.

He sighed and took Maria's hands in his. "I'm going to be in Honduras."

"You're going to Honduras next summer?" Maria frowned some more. "Well, okay. The camp will miss you, but I know you'll do good work down there, too."

"Not just next summer, Mama." He shook his head. Hope loved the way he pronounced *Mama* with the Hispanic accent. "I'm going to start being a missionary down there this fall."

Maria just looked at him.

"There's a team down there now. And they've been together for several years, but one of the families is looking into moving back stateside next year. They've had some complications with their baby and need to be closer to the doctors here. When I heard that a spot was opening up, I thought it would be the perfect opportunity to join their group for a while." Joe said it all in a rush, as if he were ripping a bandage off a wound.

"You are going, too, Hope?" Maria asked suddenly.

"No." Hope held up her hands. "I'm only here because Joe was too chicken to tell you by himself."

"Too chicken to tell your own *madre* that you're going to work for the Lord." Maria threw her napkin on the table and stormed off to the kitchen with her plate. Hope could hear more grumbling coming through the doorway, but she wasn't sure what Maria was saying because she had switched to Spanish. From the tone of it, Hope was pretty sure she didn't want to know.

"That went well," Joe said sarcastically and leaned on his elbows.

"She's going to be okay with it. I think she's just hurt you didn't tell her sooner. I mean, the fact that I knew before she did, and you barely know me ..." Hope shrugged.

"I know. I was stupid. I just couldn't figure out the timing."

Maria came back in, still muttering something about *estupido* and Honduras and *madre* as she grabbed the plates from in front of Hope and Joe and then went back to the kitchen.

"Maybe I should go ..." Hope pushed back from the table.

"Just leave me here with that Mexican thunderstorm? Thanks a lot, Hope." Joe's voice held a hint of teasing.

"In a couple of months, you're going to be missing her." Hope tried to keep herself from hoping he'd be missing someone else, too.

"I know." His reply was quiet, solemn.

"I think you're going to make a great missionary." She squeezed his hands.

He grabbed hers and didn't let go. "What makes you say so? You just pointed out I barely know you."

"But I've seen the way you teach class at church, the way you interact with kids, the way you are with others your age and older. You're just about the friendliest guy I've ever met. And who can resist that smile?" She batted her eyes at him to show she was joking with the last part.

"Obviously some can." He stared at her.

"We've been over this." Hope took her hands back. "We're headed in opposite directions."

"Maybe." Joe stood as she got ready to go.

"Tell your mom I said thanks for the great meal. I'll see you guys tomorrow."

"Be careful going home." He reached toward her again but stopped himself.

"You bet." She headed out into the hot Texas night. With Joe's admonition ringing through her head, she was cautious as she drove through the neighborhoods back toward Faith's house. Faith and Sam didn't live too far from the Hernandezes. Hope figured Maria would forgive Joe soon, if not this evening. She just had to wrap her mind around it, sort of like Hope was trying to wrap her heart around the thought of not seeing Joe after next month.

When she was back in her room, she opened her laptop and pulled up the internet. Even though it had been nice having her own mother here for a few nights, it was wonderful to have the bed back instead of the air mattress on the floor. She clicked through her emails and social media quickly in very little time and then started down the list of websites she checked every day, one for each school in a fifty-mile radius of Oxford, Mississippi.

"Come on, God. What am I supposed to do if I can't find a job?" She leaned her head back against the wall and looked up at the ceiling as if He would post an answer there. "How is this going to turn out good like Joe says it will?"

CHAPTER 18

FAITH

Faith loved her card-making group. She did. She reminded herself of this as she drove home from what had turned out to be a really tough evening. Maysie had not been able to come tonight because Kendra had come down with a fever. Six other ladies had shown up to stamp cards, though, and that part had been fun.

The hard bit had been when each lady asked Faith how she was doing. She knew they were just concerned, but sometimes concern turns into bad advice or not-so-comforting sayings. She cringed again at several of them as she drove home.

Lisa had said, "But isn't it great to know that baby won't ever have to deal with all the horrible stuff in this world? She's safe in the arms of Jesus, rest her soul."

Yes. Faith loved the idea of getting to meet her child one day when she got to Heaven. But right now, she'd much rather have that sweet baby back inside of her, growing and developing until she could hold her in her arms and rock her at night and sing lullabies and kiss boo-boos. Faith had to shake those thoughts from her head quickly or she'd have to pull over and have a good cry only two miles from home.

"Miscarriages happen all the time, dear." Annalee had patted Faith on the shoulder. "You'll get through this."

"I know it's hard right now, but the pain eases with time." Lisa had nodded.

"My cousin had a miscarriage, and she has four children now." Annalee held up four fingers.

Neither of those women had ever had a miscarriage. Faith had chewed on her tongue to keep from snapping at them that this was a child they were talking about, not just some formless blob. She had lost a child, and it hurt as much as if the baby had been born and died in her sleep or from childhood cancer or drowning in a swimming pool. She had loved this baby from the very first day she knew it existed. She hated the term *miscarriage*. It didn't speak death enough to her. Everyone just treated it like an illness to get over.

She had suffered through the well-meaning comments and suggestions, even the ones about trying again as soon as possible since it seemed like now that she could get pregnant, maybe having another child would take her mind off this one. She knew the Bible mentioned several times that men had comforted their wives after losing a baby and they had conceived with another one. They might have a point, but she really didn't want to think about it yet.

Or did she? Was God trying to show her that this was what she needed to do? Did she need to just dust herself off and try again so she could move on? She made a mental note to look up those verses when she got home.

Sam came in later that evening from a basketball meeting while she was rummaging through the drawer of his nightstand. "What are you looking for?"

"My thermometer." She moved several small basketballs with Sam's school's emblem printed on them and a pair of boxers that had been put in the wrong drawer.

Sam stood there for a moment watching her. She glanced over her shoulder to see what he was doing. The expressions on his face were not happy ones.

"Do you know where it is?" She turned to face him.

"Yes."

"Are you going to tell me?"

"No." He crossed his arms.

She frowned and started digging through the drawer below the one she had been looking in. "Fine."

"Why are you looking for it?" Sam sat on the edge of the bed.

"So we can use it again." Faith scooted over to make room for him.

"Faith, we don't need it yet."

"But Sam. Why not try again? The doctor said we could try again in a couple months. Why not start keeping track again so we'll be ready?" She held up a random picture of Sam from high school and then threw it back in the drawer. "I'm not saying go back on the Clomid and other hormones right away, but just see if maybe my body is still accepting of the idea of getting pregnant."

"The doctor said we could try again when your body is ready. It's only been a week. Only a few days since your procedure."

"It seems longer." Her hands stilled for a moment. Was it just a week ago that she had been pregnant?

"Faith." Sam pulled her away from the nightstand. "I don't know about you, but I'm not done grieving."

Faith chewed on her lip. "I know. But look."

She dragged her Bible over from where she had it open on her side of the bed. She pointed to Genesis 4:25. "And Adam knew his wife again, and she bore a son and named him Seth, 'For God has appointed another seed for me instead of Abel, whom Cain killed.'"

"Um, okay," Sam said.

"And here." Faith flipped through the pages. "Second Samuel 12:24 says, 'Then David comforted Bathsheba his wife, and went in to her and lay with her. So she bore a son, and he called his name Solomon.'"

"Okay. So, the men of the Bible slept with their wives. We

already knew that. If they hadn't, we wouldn't be here today." Sam gave a short laugh.

"Sam, don't you see? When people in the Bible lost a baby, this is what they did to comfort each other. And then, they had another baby."

Sam took the Bible out of her hands and set it on the nightstand.

She opened the third drawer down, the last one in his nightstand. He lunged past her and grabbed the basal body thermometer before she could pick it up from where it lay with several old charts from when they had been trying to get pregnant before. She reached for it, and he held it out of her grasp. She leapt up to try and grab it, but he was too tall for her.

"We. Don't. Need. It. Yet." The words came out between his clenched teeth.

"It won't hurt anything to start keeping track again." She had to control the urge to beat her fists against his chest. Why wasn't he listening to her?

"Faith, no. We're not trying anything again yet. Please stop asking." His voice had gotten louder as she kept insisting.

"But what if we miss an opportunity for another child? What if I ovulate and we don't know it? There's nothing wrong with knowing." Tears began to roll down her cheeks as she tried to get the device out of his hand again.

"No, Faith!" He threw it against the wall. It shattered, pieces scattering over the floor. "What is with you tonight?"

She tried to climb over the bed to go after the broken device, but he caught her and pulled her into his lap. She struggled for a moment, but his arms were solid—not tight enough to hurt her, but strong enough to make sure she stayed where she was. He began to rock her back and forth gently until she finally relaxed into him, her tears soaking his shirt.

"Rough night?" His voice was barely above a whisper.

"It's like no one wants to acknowledge that Moira was a real baby. Just because she was only ten and a half weeks doesn't mean she didn't have a soul." Faith sobbed into his chest.

"I know, Baby." Sam rubbed circles on her back. "I know."

"Why do people try to say things to comfort other people? They only say things that make it hurt worse."

"I don't know. Maybe it's one of Satan's tools. Humans meaning well and failing horribly." Sam continued to rock her.

She leaned back and looked at him, wiping her cheeks. "But it wouldn't hurt if we did get pregnant again right away, right? I mean, we could, right? You said you weren't ready to give up."

"Faith, there's not giving up, and then there's rushing things. I think if we start trying again too soon—or even think about it too soon—we're going to feel like this new baby is just a replacement of Moira. Not a child in itself. It will just be what Moira never got to be. And that's not fair to the child we lost. I also don't want you worrying the whole time you're pregnant *when* it happens again—and it will—if you're going to lose that child, too." Sam brushed her hair out of her face where it clung to her damp cheeks.

"So, we're not even going to get ready to try again." Her shoulders slumped.

"Honey, take time and mourn. It's okay to grieve. It's okay to feel like you just lost a loved one. You did. And if I need to dress us all in black and have you wearing a veil just to get it through to the thick-skulled women at church, we can do that. Don't rush into this. We'll try again later. Right now, let's just recover from this." His voice had risen in the middle of that speech, and Faith wondered a bit if maybe he wouldn't start fending off ladies who came up to her the next time they were at worship services.

She giggled at that mental picture.

"What's so funny?" he asked.

"I just had this image of you in my head, swinging a baseball bat at anyone who tried to get close to me at church. I think some of those women could take you."

"Hey!" He leaned to where he could look her in the eyes. "I've been working out with my boys. I could take any of those biddies." He flexed his arms so that his biceps were defined.

"I don't know." Faith shook her head. "Have you seen the size of some of those purses they carry?"

He tickled her sides in revenge, and she shrieked with mirth. She wiggled and squirmed to get away from his teasing fingers, but he still had a good grip on her, and they both ended up falling over onto the mattress. That only made them both laugh harder.

He pinned her down with his elbows and wiggled his hands in front of her. "I won't quit until you admit I'm stronger than those women."

"No!" She tried to roll over and scoot away, but that only seemed to give him more places to tickle.

"Do you give in?" He murmured right in her ear as she squealed again.

"Okay. Okay." She went completely still. "You win. You could take any of them."

He rolled off her and pulled her back into his arms. His face was inches from hers as they both lay there, recovering from the mirth. He searched her eyes for a moment before he leaned even closer. His breath tickled her skin before his lips completely closed the gap. He kissed her, gently at first and then deeper.

Even though they had gone through this together, they had both been dealing with it in their own ways for the last week. This was the first night that Faith had been whole enough to laugh again. And as he continued kissing her, she thought maybe she knew why the Bible said husbands comforted their wives this way.

CHAPTER 19

HOPE

The Fourth of July dawned beautiful and clear. Sam, Faith, and Hope joined Maysie and her husband, Gavin, and Kendra, Maria, and Joe and headed to a local park that evening. Hope ended up crammed in the back seat of Maysie's Suburban between Maria and Joe. Every time his knee brushed hers, she had to refocus on the conversation going on around her. It was the one day of the summer that camp was closed, but she didn't mind getting to spend it with Joe anyway. Once again, this week she had been paired with him and the first-grade boys. Did he bribe Steve to make that happen over and over again?

Since so many people were at the park for the fireworks show that evening, they parked quite a way from the actual entrance and had to walk. Kendra latched on to Maria. Sam and Faith strolled ahead with the blankets and some lawn chairs. Maysie and Gavin pulled the cooler full of waters and sodas. Joe and Hope ended up at the end of their train with a couple more chairs.

"Faith!" Someone called out from one of the cars they meandered past.

Faith turned and waved at a pretty woman with her family. "Hope, come here. I want you to meet Sophia."

Hope shrugged at Joe and then joined her sister.

"Sophia, this is my sister, Hope." Faith drew her arm through Hope's. "She's the teacher."

"Hope, I'm so glad to meet you." Sophia shook her hand. "I've heard so many great things about you from Faith."

"This is my friend I was telling you about that's on the school board." Faith widened her eyes at Hope as if to say, "Be nice."

As if Hope needed to be reminded to be kind to a stranger. She'd been a teacher the last few years. She knew how to put on a public face, even if she wasn't feeling friendly. Since she was in a really good mood this evening, Faith's not-so-subtle look was just insulting.

"Actually, later this week is the job fair. If you can make it, I know for a fact that several schools in the area are looking for math teachers. Including the one Sam works at." Sophia pulled something from her satchel. "Here's a brochure."

She handed Hope a flyer with the times, location, and a list of the schools involved, as well as what positions they were looking to fill. Hope gave a small smile that she hoped seemed genuine and then caught up with the rest of their group. She wasn't sure what to think about that encounter. Once again, she had been to every website of every school in her hometown area and found nothing but frustration. It was just over a month away from the first day of school and she still didn't have a job lined up.

Joe snatched the paper out of her hand as they followed the others. "Job fair, huh?"

"Yeah. But it's during camp hours, so I couldn't go anyway." Hope reached, trying to get it back from him.

"I bet Steve could find someone to fill in for you." He held it just far enough away that her attempts were futile. "I know several other counselors are taking off various hours over the next few weeks to do similar things. There's a lot of counselors who aim to be teachers." Joe's eyes skimmed the list.

"But I haven't given him any kind of notice. That's not fair to him."

"In other words, you're looking for an excuse not to go." Joe cut a glance in her direction.

"That's not what I said." Hope barely kept herself from putting her hands on her hips. They were near enough to the rest of the group now that she didn't want this conversation being overheard. All she needed was everyone else chiming in that it would be a good idea for her to attend. "Besides, what does it matter? You aren't going to be around to care where I work."

The hurt expression that crossed his face as she snatched the flyer back from him almost made her regret her words. Almost. But he wasn't being fair to her as he continued to act like he wanted a relationship even knowing he wasn't going to be in this area after August. She hurried ahead to where her sister and Sam were stopped.

Somehow despite the crowd, they managed to find a spot big enough for all of them close enough to the stage to hear the music, but also near enough to the water to have a good view of the fireworks later that evening. Hope helped Faith spread out the blankets on the ground while the guys set up the chairs around the edge for those who didn't think the grass was soft enough. Hope found a corner of the blanket and some water. Joe sat in a chair right behind her.

"It's so hot." Hope fanned herself with the flyer.

"But at least it's dry heat instead of that humid heat back east." Faith held a bottle so that Kendra could take a swig. "I swear you walk out of the house at Mama's and it feels like you're walking through a hot tub, it's so humid."

"It's not that bad. I miss the humidity. Here, I feel like I can't keep my skin from drying out." Hope pointed to her arms, which didn't look as dry as she claimed, considering the sheen of perspiration covering them.

"I sweat so much I don't think my skin can dry out." Maysie

laughed. "I didn't realize there was such a difference in climate between here and Mississippi."

"Not that extreme. Just different." Hope shrugged. "The temperatures don't get quite as high back home."

"But the 90 percent humidity makes up for the five- to ten-degree difference." Faith scrunched up her face.

"So, you're both happy where you normally live." Joe broke in. "Sounds good. How about that baseball team?"

Hope refused to look over her shoulder at him. She knew exactly what he was trying to do. He had changed the subject to keep her and Faith from beginning one of their sister squabbles. She quit fanning and looked at the flyer again. There were at least four different math positions listed. That was four more than she had found back in Mississippi.

"I can go in for you that day if you want to go to the job fair." Faith's quiet voice interrupted Hope's thoughts.

Hope quickly folded the paper and stuck it in her pocket. "I don't know. I'm not sure you could stand putting up with Joe all day."

"Hey!" He nudged her with his foot. "I'm the best co-counselor at camp, and you know it."

"I sort of miss Tessa." Hope glanced over her shoulder. "She was a lot quieter."

Everyone laughed. Some band on the stage was playing their version of a patriotic medley. Hope turned her view in their direction to avoid having to continue the conversation. The sky darkened little by little and several kids in the area waved glow sticks. Occasionally there would be a "pop, pop, pop" of firecrackers going off from various boys' hands around the park. Multiple ice cream vendors walked their carts through the throng of people, hawking fudge bars and rocket pops.

Joe followed one and came back with the red, white, and blue popsicles for everyone. Hope took hers gladly. A gentle breeze lifted her ponytail off her neck and cooled her for a minute before moving on to the next person. The wind down here took some getting used to. Sometimes it was like that breeze, playful and calm. Other times it almost knocked a person over. Sort of like her relationship with Joe.

"Here, Mama, you take this chair." Joe stood and offered his hand to Maria where she had been shifting next to Hope. He pulled her up as if she weighed no more than one of their second-grade boys and helped her settle in the canvas seat.

His tall frame slid down next to Hope as the streaks of pink turned a shade hotter in the sky. She pretended she didn't notice, but every inch of her body was aware of just how close his was to her. She slapped at a mosquito and rubbed some more repellent on her legs and arms. The darkening evening brought not only the fireworks show, but also unwanted pests.

After a dramatic musical introduction, the first few rockets shot up in the sky. The crowd grew quieter as all listened to the songs and the explosions. Shivers ran down Hope's arms as the theatrical lights display lit up the night.

"Sort of reminds me of the way I felt when I kissed you the other night," Joe whispered in her ear.

Bigger tremors traversed her spine. Had he really just said that? A quick glance showed him watching her instead of the pyrotechnics. She hurried to turn her attention back to the sky. Why did he have to play with her heart like that?

He shifted so that his shoulder was slightly behind her and she could lean back against him for a better angle. Her stubbornness made her wait until the next song started before she gave in and took advantage of that. Why did he have to feel so strong and safe and secure? Why did something so good have to have such lousy timing?

Faith leaned against Sam in a similar fashion. Maysie and Gavin had Kendra between them, the toddler vacillating between jumping up and down and covering her eyes. The music crescendoed and moved into the "1812 Overture." Fireworks larger than before started exploding one right after another, hardly giving their eyes time to adjust to the dark before lighting up the sky again. As the song ended, one final blast made it almost as bright as day, and then all was quiet and dark.

People all over the park cheered. Kids waved their glow sticks and sparklers around. Smoke hovered over the area like a blanket. Slowly, Hope sat up and away from Joe's arms. She helped the others gather their belongings and then started the trek back to the car. Maria walked right beside Hope and gave her a hug from the side.

"I see the way he looks at you. He's smitten." Her voice was quiet, as if she were sharing a secret.

Hope looked at the petite woman. "It doesn't matter. Our paths will part ways at the end of the summer."

"Only if you let them," Maria said.

Hope didn't even try to pay attention to the conversation going on around her as they drove back to the church building, where everyone had met. She relished the feel of Joe being pressed against her side. And she thought about what Maria had said.

~

Faith

Faith decided it was time to start getting everything straightened out for preschool this fall. Originally, she had not planned to teach again this coming year, but when she lost her reason for staying home, she and Sam both agreed that it would be a good way to keep her mind occupied. Her director had been thrilled to have one of her favorite teachers back.

Faith sorted through the three tubs of leftover arts-and-crafts supplies and story-telling props she had brought home. She set aside the visual aids and bulletin board pieces she could use again, removing staples and sticky tack as she went. Sheets of construction paper were gone through to determine whether or not they were large enough to actually use in a future project. She held up pieces where she had cut the kids' hands out for various projects last year and compared their tiny sizes to her hands. She would never get to do that with Moira.

In her accordion file that she kept for preschool stuff, she filed away coloring pages and patterns for the different months. Since she had been doing this for three years now, she had her curriculum pretty much set and just had to do the prep work for each craft instead of also planning the various activities. Occasionally, she would find an idea she liked better and would add it to her collection, but for the most part, she had found enough different projects to keep her two-year-olds happy during the year and their moms pleased, too.

Towards the bottom of the last tub, Faith discovered some scrapbooking supplies that she had used to put together a little memory book for each child at the end of the last school year. She picked them up and sorted through the various pieces left in the big pack of paper she had purchased for that project. In the back of the tablet were some baby-themed sheets, and she paused. Laid out where she could see them all together, an idea started to form in her head.

Faith got up and dug through a stack of pictures she had printed out earlier in the summer until she found what she was looking for. It didn't take her long to locate some solid paper and her glue widget and scissors, along with several pens and a paper cutter. With practiced hands, she started arranging and laying out various pages for a scrapbook.

The first page she put together centered around a picture of her pregnancy test that had finally shown two lines instead of just one. She paired it with a photo of her holding it up, a huge smile pasted on her face, like she had never been happier. In truth, she hadn't. Would she ever find that joy again? She wrote the date out beside the snapshots and the words *Finally pregnant!* She pressed down the edges and included a stamp about dreams being fulfilled.

The second page was the picture she had forced her husband to take of her at a side angle so she could watch her belly grow week by week. Of course, that first week her stomach had still been flat, but she had looked forward to seeing it expand over the pregnancy. She did several pages of the weekly belly photos with dates and *Week 3, Week 4,* ... with the waist measurements she had taken. As she looked back over the snapshots, it was obvious that her belly had indeed started to swell by the end.

On the last page, Faith wasn't sure what to do. Her eyes caught on the roll of ultrasound pictures they had gotten shortly before losing Moira. She snipped the clearest one free and centered it on the page, then pulled out a calligraphy pen and neatly wrote, "Moira Angela McCreary, due date December 20, lost to us June 25, forever in our hearts." It wasn't a tombstone. The baby hadn't been big enough to need a proper burial or funeral. But it was her way of trying to have some closure.

"I'll see you in Heaven, little girl." She gently ran her fingers over the scrapbook she had started putting together. "And won't it be a joke on us if you are a boy?"

CHAPTER 20

HOPE

Hope paused and took a deep breath before she entered the gymnasium. She wore a pantsuit, and her hair was pulled back neatly in a French braid. Her hands clasped a folder with twenty-five copies of her résumé. The air conditioning hit her as she walked through the doors and into the cacophony of about fifty different quiet conversations. Despite the fact that a tarp covered the basketball court, the voices echoed off the hard surfaces of the building. The familiar smell of stinky tennis shoes greeted her even though school had been out for several months. She accepted a map from the table inside the doorway to show her where each school was located.

The gym swarmed with people who had the same purpose in mind. And there weren't all young teachers, either. Some of the people passing around résumés were old enough to have been her teachers in high school—not that she was old enough to make them ancient or anything. Still. It made her pause because that meant even established teachers were being laid off, not just the ones who had only been in the field for a little while like she had. Did she even have a shot? Was she wasting her time?

"I'm here anyway. Might as well meet some schools." She

straightened her shoulders and approached the first table on her right. "Here goes nothing."

The first school was a bust, as they were not looking for any math teachers. The second was farther south in Austin than she would want to work, so she didn't chat with them more than a few moments. The next one, however, sounded more promising. They had spots open for several middle school math teachers. She mentally crossed her fingers and gave her best smile.

"So where are you coming from again?" The lady took Hope's résumé.

"Mississippi." Hope didn't want her home state to scare off potential jobs, so she hurried on. "I've been there for two years, but my sister lives in this area, and she told me about the job fair today."

"Have you already started looking into getting a Texas teaching license? I assume you're still certified to teach in Mississippi?" The woman continued to scan over Hope's information.

Hope grimaced. "I haven't yet. Honestly, I didn't realize I was even going to have this chance while I was down here visiting her until the other day. But I'm willing to do what I need to do to make it work."

The woman nodded. "Well, your résumé looks good. Looks like you've got your masters as well?"

"Yes. I went ahead and got my masters right after I graduated so I could have that extra bit of education under my belt and be a better teacher right from the start."

"Two years at Buckley High. Just algebra or anything else?"

"I did teach a class of trigonometry and have taught geometry as well over the last two years. I could definitely handle statistics if I needed to, but I prefer algebra over the other subjects in math." Hope tried not to think about what the statistics of getting a teaching position for this fall would be.

"Well, let me tell you what you need to do to go about getting a Texas teaching license, and at least then you'll have a better answer at the other tables." The lady laid aside Hope's papers and skimmed through an accordion file until she found a sheet with the information she was looking for. The interview had ended rather abruptly. Hope wondered if it was because she wasn't certified to teach in Texas or if the lady just plain didn't like her from the start. She tried not to let it get to her as she listened to what the woman was saying about transferring a certification.

"You'll have to pay around two hundred dollars up front and make sure you get all your transcripts as well as copies of your certification to the state now. Then, once all that goes through, they'll let you teach here for a year, as long as you take the requisite tests during that time. It's not too hard, but it does have to be done just to make sure you meet all our state requirements. Teaching requirements differ from state to state."

Was that a jab at how "dumb" Mississippi was considered to be? Once again, Hope tried to swallow her pride and not let the woman get to her. She thanked her instead and moved on to the next table, the new sheet of paper clutched to her chest with the rest of her résumés.

After several more tables of schools not looking for math teachers, she met with a gentleman who gladly accepted her résumé when he found out what subject she taught. "We're actually looking for two different math teachers. We need junior high as well as one that can teach high school, including trig."

"I'm certified to teach math grades 8 through 12." She nodded.

"I see you're from Mississippi." He continued to look over the paper she had handed him. "When did you move here?"

"I actually haven't yet. I'm living with my sister this summer and working out at Camp TwinCreeks, but she told me about this job fair, and I worked it out where I could come, just to see if the education market is better here than back home." Did that make her sound flaky? Like she was just looking on a whim?

"So, your certification is actually in Mississippi?" he asked.

"Yes, but I have the information I need to be able to change it to Texas. I'd be more than willing to work on getting it transferred as soon as I could." Hope was now ecstatic she had talked with the other lady first and knew more about the process. She just hoped she sounded as confident as she was trying to.

One of the last tables was covered in a dark green tablecloth, and she was greeted with warm smiles as she walked up to it. She went through her introduction and what she taught and was told that they were in fact in need of a math teacher. She glanced at the brochure they handed her of their school history and pay scale and noticed that it was a Christian school. She glanced again and realized it was the one where Sam worked.

"Do you know Sam McCreary?" she asked.

"Yes. He's one of our coaches and a history teacher," the principal, Ms. Waverly, said. "How do you know him?"

"He's my brother-in-law." Hope gave a small grin.

"He's a great teacher." Ms. Waverly motioned with her hands. "We're so glad to have him working with us. Is that why you're here?"

"I actually had forgotten that you would be here. I'm here to see what's available because I was in the area this summer, and my school back in Mississippi had to do some cutbacks. I was the last one hired, so ..."

"Well, I'm sure we'd love to have you. And since we're a private school, you wouldn't even have to get your certification changed over as quickly as with a public school. As long as you have a degree in what you're teaching, that's all you need." Ms. Waverly pulled her glasses off and let them dangle from the chain around her neck. "Obviously, we're all for you being a certified teacher, but we could hire you without it and let you work toward that while you work for us."

Hope had to admit, for the first time in her life she was actually tempted by a Christian school. She usually gave the argument that public schools needed good Christian teachers and she should be out teaching among the "heathens" whenever she and Sam had the discussion about which was better. But her situation had changed just enough over the last few months that she might consider accepting an offer from a small Christian school if they made one.

"This is your pay scale?" She skimmed through their brochure.

"Yes. We try to maintain a pay scale that is around 80% of what you would be making if you were to work for the public schools. Some years the budget is a bit tighter than others, obviously, but since you have two years of experience, you would start out around here." Ms. Waverly slipped her glasses back on. She pointed to a number on the page that was several thousand below what Hope was used to bringing in.

"Wow." Hope's eyes widened a bit. She hoped it sounded like a good wow and not a "How on earth do people live on just that much a year?" wow. Her eyes scanned a little farther down the page until she could see the number next to the amount of time Sam had been teaching. His wasn't very much higher than hers.

"Of course, with your master's degree, too, we'd add a couple of years' experience for that." Ms. Waverly motioned farther down the page. Obviously, Hope's wow had sounded more like the second one than she meant for it to.

They chatted for a little bit longer and then Hope moved on. She finished up the last table and left, not certain how the day had gone. She had at least talked to every school present in the gymnasium. She had left a résumé with twelve different schools and had come out knowing how to switch her teaching license if the need arose. However, she had also missed a day of work and her feet were sore from wearing high heels for the last few hours instead of the sneakers she had grown accustomed to at camp.

She wearily drove back to Faith's house and let herself in. Sam was home and working on fixing something on the kitchen sink when she came through. She slipped off her shoes at the counter and picked them up to carry the rest of the way.

"How'd it go?" His voice came out muffled from under the cabinet.

"Not sure." She tugged at the end of her braid. "I spoke to several different schools, left résumés with at least twelve of them, and really have no idea what any of them thought of me. I talked to your school, too."

"Oh? Ms. Waverly?"

"Yeah. She seems really nice." Hope leaned against a stool. "I think she was more interested in me than I was in her school, though."

"Still hung up on not teaching at a Christian school?" Sam sat up to look at her.

"It's not the school. It's the lack of a decent paycheck." Hope made a face. "I don't know how you guys can live on so little."

"Our life isn't about the money. We have enough to be comfortable, we live within our means, and I feel like I'm doing the best job I can for kids who need me. Christian schools need good teachers, too, you know."

"I know." Hope shrugged. "I guess I feel a bit guilty about how I've been mooching off you two all summer, though. I knew your school wouldn't pay as much, but I didn't realize ..." She held the brochure up with the pay scale on it.

"It helps that I get the coach's version of that. And Faith brings in a little each month from selling her stamps. And during the school year we've got her preschool check, too. We're not suffering just because you're sleeping under our roof. Besides, lately you seem to be eating more with Joe than with us." Sam winked.

Hope wrinkled her nose. "I know."

"He's not that bad." Sam laughed.

"That's the problem." Hope walked down the hallway to change into more comfortable clothes.

CHAPTER 21

FAITH

"And you have the numbers where we can be reached if you need anything." Faith touched the piece of paper stuck to the front of the refrigerator. "Although we should have our cell phones with us no matter what, so you probably won't need these numbers."

"Faith, I'm a big girl. I've lived by myself before, and I can do it again while you're gone for a few days. I'll be fine." Hope crossed her heart.

"I know. I'm just not used to someone still being here when we're gone, I guess." Faith looked around the kitchen again.

"Ready?" Sam came in from the garage. "I've got everything loaded."

Faith chewed her bottom lip as she gave one more glance around the room. She always had the impression that she was forgetting something when they went on a trip. Unfortunately, it usually didn't strike her what had been left behind until after they had been on the road for a while. She nodded since she couldn't think of another reason to not leave.

"You two have a good time." Hope waved from the doorway.

Faith grinned at Sam as they backed her SUV out of the driveway and headed south toward San Antonio. It had been a while since they had gotten away, just the two of them, not to go see family or on a school trip. So, when Sam had decided since it was their seventh anniversary and they had some time, they might as well take a few days and go do something fun, she had agreed. Even though they had lived in Texas for over five years, they had not taken the time to play the tourist in San Antonio, so that was the plan.

As they passed the outlet mall in San Marcos on the way down, she pointed out the window. "Maybe we could stop there on our way back."

"We'll see." He had been quiet since they got in the car, mostly just humming along with the music.

"This was a good idea, huh?" Faith laid her hand over his on the center console. "Us getting away for a few days."

He squeezed her fingers. "I know I needed it."

"You'd think it would take longer than seven years for a marriage to feel like this." She nibbled her bottom lip.

"What?" He shot her a sideways glance before returning his attention to the highway.

"When we first got married, we swore we would never let ourselves get out of the honeymoon stage. We wanted to always feel so in love and enamored of each other." She ran her thumb over the back of his hand. "But we sort of forgot that along the way. When we decided to try to have kids. And then everything we went through to do that. And then, this summer …"

"As much as I enjoyed the honeymoon stage of our relationship, I probably wouldn't go back."

"No?"

"No." He shook his head. "Our love is deeper now. It's been through more. Weathered some storms and come out stronger, in my opinion. That doesn't mean we don't need to continue to work on our marriage, take trips like this just the two of us and remember why we like each other." He shot her a grin. "But I'd rather have the love we have now than the one we started out with."

She thought about that as they continued their journey. Everyone told them at the beginning that the first couple of years of a marriage were the hardest. Now that she had been through seven, she wasn't sure she completely agreed, although there had been a few tumultuous occasions in that first stretch when they had still been learning to live with each other. But she could also see Sam's point. She was more in love with him today than she had been back when they started.

Less than an hour later, they were parked at the hotel and checked into their room. He'd gotten one with a little kitchenette in it since they were going to be there for several days. Out the window, bits of the River Walk peeked through between the buildings. She let the drapes fall back into place and turned to find Sam watching her.

"So, what's the plan for the rest of the day?" she asked.

"I don't know." He gave a small shrug. "We can go see the Alamo, go to Sea World, or go explore the River Walk. Or there's the zoo that you had mentioned wanting to see. Or some caves not too far away."

"It may be too hot for the Alamo right now." She wrinkled her nose. "But we probably have enough time to go play at Sea World, right?"

"Sure. Let's go let some fish splash us." He offered her his arm and escorted her back out to the car.

In addition to all the animals, the park also had a couple of roller coasters. Faith hadn't ridden one in years, so Sam had to coax her into line with him. As the cars went up, up, up to the peak of a huge drop, she remembered why she had sworn off these rides back in college. She screamed and grabbed Sam's arm as the machine whipped her around and up and down and back to the start again.

"Never again, Sam McCreary." Faith's legs were still shaking as he helped her up onto the sidewalk.

"But what if our future kids want to ride?"

"They will have to go with someone else. I will gladly sit and wait while you put your life on the line." She shook her head. "I'm too old for that."

"Okay. No more coasters." He hugged her to his side. "At least not today."

They held hands as they strolled through the exhibit of poisonous sea creatures. After a snow cone, they watched the sea lion show and laughed as the cold water splashed up on them when the animals jumped in the pool. The walrus who could do sit-ups almost stole the show from the silly sea lions.

They stood and admired the dolphins for a while. Sam paid for a few fish and held one up so a dolphin could snatch it out of his hand. He offered one to Faith and she wrinkled her nose at it. He grabbed her hand and wrapped it around the little fish, and then helped her dangle it over the water so the dolphin could jump up and snack. Faith laughed and wiped her hand on his shirt.

A family with two young kids came closer to take their turn of offering fish to the mammals, causing Faith to pause. The little girl gingerly took the fish, and then the daddy held her over the water so the dolphins could reach. The child giggled with glee as the nose touched her hand and snatched the snack. Without thinking, Faith put a hand to her abdomen, where the baby had been growing just three weeks before. Sam pulled her into a hug and steered her farther down the path.

"Someday," he whispered.

They couldn't have a complete day at Sea World without seeing a whale, of course. As they entered the stadium to see his show, they glanced at the various seats left. Most of them were in the splash zone.

"Maybe if we sit at the very top of the splash zone, it won't be so bad." She pointed toward the higher bleachers. He shrugged and joined her on the last row marked in red.

As the show progressed, they exchanged a look as Shamu entered the pool. Everyone knew whales were huge, but seeing one in person … that put a whole new perspective on things. The trainers had him swim around the pool. Too late, Faith noticed the swell in the water that followed him as he continued to circumnavigate the perimeter. The seven-foot wave crashed over the side of the pool, soaking them in cold salt water. Even though the weather had been warm that day, she shivered as the moisture seeped into her clothes.

"Top of the splash zone is still the splash zone." Sam pulled at his wet shirt, grimacing as his tongue tasted the saltiness on his lips.

They both laughed as they exited the arena after the show. They were wetter now than when they had ridden the ride that took them to the top and then back down into the water to splash them. Faith wrung out the bottom of her t-shirt as they walked to another area to see the penguins. The sun felt nice on her chilled skin.

"Maybe penguins should have been before whales." Sam gave a theatrical shiver as they walked through the icy building.

"Obviously, we should have planned this better." She rubbed at the goose bumps on her arms.

"Now we'll know for when we bring our kids back in the future." He put an arm around her and snuggled her close until they got outside again.

She had to admire his persistence in saying, "when," as he referred to future children. She still struggled with that, more than she cared to admit.

After a turn on the 3-D theatre ride that made them feel like they were on a real pirate ship and watching the trick skiers for a little while, they decided they had done just about all they wanted to at this place and headed for the exit. Back at the hotel, after a shower and change of clothes, they were ready to head down to the River Walk to find something to eat. The crowds of people swarming the narrow area on either side of the water convinced them both they didn't want to walk very far this evening.

They settled at a little bistro table right beside the river, under a colorful umbrella. The scents of barbeque and Tex-Mex hung heavy on the air as they waited for their own brisket plates to be brought out. They watched the various tour groups cruising up and down the river and could hear bits and pieces of the history as the guides narrated the trip.

"Want to go on one of those?" Sam asked.

"Maybe tomorrow." Faith leaned back in her seat. "I think Sea World wore me out."

He nodded.

Even though the sky was turning dark with evening, the lights along the River Walk were bright, and there was almost a fiesta atmosphere in the air. People walked along, doing some shopping or trying out various restaurants. Others just strolled by, enjoying the scenery and sights.

"This almost feels like a second honeymoon." Faith lifted a bite of beef to her mouth. "I needed this trip."

"I thought you might." He took a swig of his tea.

"What about you? You said earlier you needed a getaway, too."

"With you? I'm always up for getting away with you." He winked.

Even after being married for seven years now, he could still make her feel cherished and wanted. She held hands with him across the table and let the peace of the day fill her heart. They hadn't had a real vacation like this in probably five years. Yes, their love was stronger now, but he was still the playful, sweet guy she had originally crushed on in college almost ten years before.

"Do you think you needed the trip as much as I did?" Faith asked. "When we were planning it, you kept saying it was for me or for us. I don't remember you saying anything about it being for you, too."

"I know this summer hasn't been the easiest on you. With losing Moira ..." His voice broke a little as he said the name. "And then with having to put up with Hope's dramatic ups and downs on top of everything, you needed a break. And I needed time with just the two of us, focused on our relationship and not just the things happening lately."

"I'm sorry, Sam. I know this summer hasn't been particularly easy for you, either. And maybe I've made it harder, especially when ... well ... when I was wallowing in my self-pity." She stared at the scalloped pattern on the table for a long moment. "And I keep thinking, what if ..."

He waited for her to continue.

"What if I hadn't insisted on painting the room, or carrying stuff that was so heavy, or working that week at camp. What if I had started vitamins earlier or stayed off my feet more. Or what if I hadn't let Hope come down this summer after all ... would I still be pregnant?" She choked back a sob at the last question.

"What-ifs are nothing but speculation. And honestly, none of that probably had anything to do with the miscarriage."

"I know that in my head." Faith gave a slight nod. "It's my heart that keeps wondering."

"I know." He squeezed her hand.

They paid the bill and walked the River Walk for a little longer. He waved down one of the carriage rides and convinced the driver to take them all the way back to their hotel. Faith snuggled into his side despite the heat that remained in the city. She loved that she had married a man who could still surprise her with little things. He might say he wasn't romantic, but that didn't mean he couldn't pull it off every now and then.

CHAPTER 22

HOPE

"Why does it feel so much hotter today?" Hope eased down on the side of the pool during the last swimming period of the day. It was the week after the job fair, and she was trying not to think about the fact that she hadn't heard anything from any of the schools, not even Sam's. She dipped her feet into the water, grateful that it was still fairly cool despite the sweltering air.

"It's muggy today." Joe stood waist-deep in the water. The boys were eating it up to have him in the pool with them. They climbed on his back and laughed as he tossed them off into another section away from other kids.

One of Hope's favorite boys swam over and hung on her legs. She swished him around for a while until her legs started to get tired. When she gave up on moving her legs around, he tried to get her attention by splashing at her. Instead, she slid into the pool with him, clothes and all. The water felt good against her hot skin.

"Mugginess doesn't usually affect me like this." Her voice sounded whinier than she wanted it to, but she was miserable.

"Maybe you finally got used to the drier heat here." Joe gave a grin that showed her he was teasing.

She moved back up to the side of the pool again to get away from the boys who thought it would be fun to climb all over her, too. "Ms. Hope, no fair. Come back in the water!"

"Go climb on Mr. Joe," she said. "He likes it."

He gave her a dirty look and then came her way. With a wave of water, he lifted himself to the side of the pool beside her. His t-shirt clung to his chest and arms, displaying his defined muscles. Hope looked away and readjusted her saturated clothing to make sure she wasn't showing off as much as he had.

After a couple more minutes of listening to the boys beg for the counselors to get back in the water, Joe suggested a new game and sent the kids to the other side of the pool. Hope studied the sky in the distance. It looked darker than usual. A breeze blew past her and brought a touch of coolness to her wet skin.

"So, Joe." She cut him a sideways peek. "Is Joe short for anything?"

"It's a Bible name." He kept his attention on the boys.

"Joseph?" She guessed the first one that came to mind.

"Nope."

"Joshua?"

"Nope."

She frowned a bit. "I know there's tons of names in the Bible that start with 'j' but I can't think of any more names Joe could be short for."

He glanced at her and then quietly said, "Josiah."

She leaned a bit closer to him to make sure she heard right. "What?"

"Josiah." He repeated the name slightly louder this time.

"Like the king in the Old Testament?"

"Yes."

"That's an interesting name." She tilted her head. "I don't think I've ever heard of anyone being named Josiah."

"Not many people are, but my parents wanted me to grow up and do what God wanted me to do, and they thought that a king who would do such things was a good one to name their son after."

"Quite a lot to live up to." She meant it as a compliment to his parents for picking out the name of such a good king. From his facial expression, he obviously disagreed.

"It is a lot of pressure, but I also know that other people are named after other great historical figures. They don't always live up to their namesake, either." He shrugged. "A name is just a name. The person wearing it is who gives it value."

"I think you live up to it very well. Faith and I have Bible names, too." Hope offered an appeasement.

Joe laughed. "I never really thought about that before. Did your mom name you after I Corinthians 13?"

"Not really, but that was a family joke when we were growing up. We always said we couldn't have a little sister because then she would be named Charity and could use that verse against us."

"'Now abide these three: faith, hope and charity. And the greatest of these is charity.'" Joe quoted. "Nice."

"It works." She smirked.

"Interesting how you're both named the thing you seem to struggle the most with." Joe pulled his legs out of the water.

Hope started to ask what that meant when he pointed in the distance to where she had been watching the sky earlier. "I think I figured out why it's so muggy this afternoon."

She followed the direction of his finger and looked over at the horizon just in time to see a flash of lightning streak across the gray sky. A boom of thunder quickly followed. Several of the kids paused, and the lifeguards stood up and blew their whistles. They had been in the pool for only fifteen minutes, but this was not safe weather to be out in.

Hope hurried the kids as best she could to get them back to the dressing room. Joe unlocked it and sent them in with instructions to change as quickly as possible. Hope continued to watch the sky as she waited for the boys to finish getting dressed. She told them to just hang their towels inside instead of on the clothes line behind the dressing room as the first drops of rain plopped to the ground.

"Line up right against the wall inside, boys," Joe said. "Hurry. We need to get to the main building."

Hope huddled inside the doorway to avoid getting wetter as the sky opened up and let loose in a downpour. She exchanged glances with Joe before looking back outside to see another flash of lightning. The boys shrieked. A glimpse across the room showed at least five more campers who were still half-naked. "Come on, guys! Get dressed! The sooner you get dressed, the sooner we can get out of here and into the other building where we can have fun."

After five more minutes, everyone was clothed and ready to go. Hope moved to let Joe lead the boys through the rain. They dodged under the overhangs as much as they could, but Hope was pretty sure she was wetter now than when she had been in the pool a few minutes before. Hope breathed a sigh of relief as they joined the semi-organized chaos in the main building. Another roll of thunder clapped overhead, and Hope steered the kids farther inside.

It was miserably stuffy, even with the doors open, but it was the safest place on campus. Steve was up front, trying to get everyone calm enough that he could organize an activity for all the younger kids. The older kids soon left to make their way to one of the other pavilions, where they could still be relatively dry but also have more room to spread out. Joe brought out the stereo and started flipping through the mp3 player the camp kept for their music needs.

Soon, a country music song blasted through the din. Steve urged the kids to get up and had several counselors up front with him to lead a line dance. Hope watched for a few minutes from the side and encouraged the boys to join in. She had never line danced and wasn't sure she knew how to do it even if the moves seemed fairly easy.

Joe joined their group and started performing the various steps. He made it look like a natural and simple thing to do. Some of the boys followed his example. Hope continued to watch until he grabbed her arm and pulled her into the dancing mob.

"Like this." He pointed to his feet. "Left, right, left. Right, left, right. Kick, kick."

She haltingly followed his lead and started to figure out the patterns. Most of the rest of the first-grade boys jumped in when they saw both of their counselors dancing, too. Joe grinned at her as she kicked wrong on the last note. She shrugged and wiped her sweaty forehead on her sleeve.

A song with a cha-cha rhythm came on next, and Joe jumped right in with the rest of the group as they danced around. "Just follow the instructions. It tells you what to do."

Hope listened to the music. The musician indeed had turned his song into a list of dance steps, telling the listeners to jump and slide and cha-cha. It was almost like a modern version of a square dance.

Hope was sure she looked as jerky in her movements as most of the kids around her, but she tried to follow the directions. Joe, of course, made it look as smooth as butter, and his cha-cha showed his Latino heritage like nothing else she had seen him do that summer. She caught herself just watching him move and had to remind herself that the boys were observing her, and she should be dancing, too.

After three more songs that had them doing all sorts of silly moves, including "shake your tail feathers," Hope was elated when Steve called an end to the dance party. Her legs were more tired than usual from being up on her toes to shuffle and kick and cha-cha. She collapsed with the boys on the concrete floor, glad to watch the silly cartoons Steve put on for the last half hour of camp. The rain was still coming down outside, but the sky had lightened up, and the lightning and thunder had moved on.

"You good? I've got to go move buses up." Joe leaned down close to her.

She turned to find him only inches away from her face. She swallowed. "Fine. Go on."

If her accelerated pulse rate was any indicator, she needed to think harder about what Maria had said on the Fourth of July because her feelings for Josiah Hernandez were only getting deeper and not lessening. She tried to focus on the characters on the screen and the laughter of the boys around her instead of the boy who had just left the building to drive the buses through the mud.

She didn't remember until that evening that she had wanted to ask him what he meant about her struggling with her name. What had he meant? Did she truly have a problem with hope?

She glanced at her phone one last time before bed to make sure Faith hadn't tried to call. A voice mail alert blinked in the top corner. As she listened to it, all thoughts of Joe faded, replaced by something she had just about given up on.

CHAPTER 23

⚜

FAITH

Faith dreamed of a little girl. She and Sam had taken her to Sea World but lost her somewhere between the penguins and the whales. Everywhere she looked, she couldn't find the child, and she kept calling out for her.

"Moira!"

"Faith, wake up." Sam brushed the hair back from her face and caressed her arms.

Faith slowly opened her eyes and then sat straight up in the bed, frantically looking around the room. As she woke up and realized it had been only a nightmare, she slumped over and sobbed. Sam just rubbed her back and crooned soothing words she didn't hear over the sound of her broken heart.

"We lost her, Sam." She swiped at her tears.

"It was just a dream." He pulled her tight. "It's okay."

"It's not okay." Faith shook her head. "I lost our little girl."

∞

THE NEXT MORNING Faith awoke to the smell of coffee. She stretched and opened her eyes. It took her a moment to realize she wasn't in her own bed. She rolled over and found Sam watching her from a chair by the window. He held a steaming mug in his hands.

"Hey." His voice was soft.

"Hey."

He set his cup aside and came over to her. "You okay?"

Faith slid up the mattress so she could lean against the headboard. "I'm okay. I guess I should apologize for last night, for keeping you from sleeping."

"It's what I'm here for." He squeezed her arm. "I'm more worried about you right now. You haven't had a dream like that in several years."

Faith had suffered through nightmares and insomnia after they had been trying to conceive for two and a half years. It was a period of time she referred to in her journal as her "dark period." She had been struggling to maintain her faith in God, a faith she thought was strong enough to face anything this world could throw at her. Instead, the world had proved her theory wrong.

She had struggled most with well-meaning fellow Christians who would make comments in the class like, "If you pray for something long enough, God will give it to you—that's what it means about the persistent widow." Or, "Well, it says right here that 'God works all things for good to those who love the Lord,' so no matter what happens in your life, you know He's just using this time to bring about something better." None of that had been comforting to her. She had begged and pleaded with God for a child, and He kept answering with, "No."

The moment she realized that if God were to end the world the next day and take all the Christians to Heaven, she wasn't ready to go … that was the moment she realized she had a problem. After all, how could she be ready to leave this world before she had gotten to be a mommy? She had mixed up her priorities in life and had put being a mother ahead of serving her Lord. It had not been easy to change her thinking and her mindset, but she had striven and worked at it. And then, earlier this year, she thought God had blessed her for it by answering her prayers with, "Yes."

Now, her miscarriage had shaken her faith that she had thought was stronger than ever. It seemed it had even shaken it more than she had known because once again she was waking up with terrors in the middle of the night. She gave Sam what she hoped was a reassuring smile.

"I'm okay. I promise. Not nearly as bad as last time." She patted his hand. "I won't let myself go that low again."

Faith couldn't let herself get back to that dark period. Sure, she was upset and hurt and sad, but that didn't mean she was ready to go back down that road, right? Wasn't her faith stronger now?

"Ready for another fun-filled day of San Antonio?" he asked.

"I will be after a cup of coffee." She mentally gave herself a shake and sent her husband a smile.

They started at the Alamo since they figured that was the stop with the least amount of shade and they really didn't want to be out in the extreme July heat later in the day. It was amazing to Faith how the mission that had housed one of the biggest battles in Texas history was now completely surrounded by modern buildings and businesses deep in the heart of San Antonio. Sam soaked up the history and dragged her along with him. She tried to talk him into a Davy Crockett coonskin cap, but he wasn't interested.

From there, they went to the zoo. Hand in hand, they moseyed past lions and tigers and elephants. They examined the birds and monkeys and stared at the hippopotamus for a while. She was hanging out under water to avoid the heat that saturated the air. Faith almost wished she could join the huge water horse.

The fun little restaurant in the middle of the zoo provided a perfect lunch spot where they sat under the shade of several trees and watched other families around them. There were kids everywhere. Faith gave Sam a smile as he looked at her, a worried expression on his face.

"I'm okay, Sam. Promise. I mean, I still wish, obviously, but I'm not going to burst into tears or anything." Faith tossed a tomato at him.

"I'm sorry. I guess I'm not helping, am I?" He picked at a breadstick left on his plate.

"We both agreed a long time ago that our job is to worry about each other." Faith grinned. "You're just doing your job."

"You really are doing okay, though?" He motioned around them. "I didn't think about how many kids would be at these places we've been visiting."

"We can't exactly avoid every place there might be children for the rest of our lives, Sam." Faith reached over and brushed a strand of hair back off his forehead. "No matter what happens in our lives, if we have children in the future or not, we have to face this. I will go back to work at the preschool and love on other people's children. You will go back to school this fall and teach other people's children. If Joe and Hope can ever figure out what they're doing and get together, they might have children down the road that you know we'll love. And it's not going to be easy. But we'll get through it together."

"I still believe we'll have children, too." He pressed his forehead to hers.

"I'm trying to believe."

"Together, huh?" He pressed a kiss to her skin. "Okay. Let's go on together."

They finished walking through the zoo and headed back toward the hotel. After parking the car, they made their way across the few blocks back down to the River Walk. Sam's suggestion that it would be at least slightly cooler down by the water turned out to be right. They spent the afternoon meandering in and out of various little kitschy shops and treating themselves to an ice cream sundae in the middle. Sam paid for their passage on one of the river tours, and they climbed on board the little boat to be ferried up and down the narrow waterway and learn the history.

Sam pointed out various historical things and Faith enjoyed the architecture all around them. The city had actually rerouted the river to form the River Walk and had created this little oasis in the middle of the concrete and steel. On this hot afternoon, Faith was grateful for the cool breeze off the water and the shade of the buildings around them.

They grabbed dinner and headed out to Wednesday evening Bible study. Sam had looked up a nearby congregation and printed out a map and times so they wouldn't be late. Several couples greeted them as they entered and found a spot toward the back of the auditorium.

The discussion in the class started in James 1, talking about finding joy in trials. Then, the teacher reminded them of Romans 8:28, saying "all things work together for good."

Here we go again. Faith shrank into herself, waiting to hear the same old lesson on how there was something good in every bad thing in life. *Not in losing my baby, God. There's no good in that.*

Then, the teacher moved on to 2 Corinthians 1:3-7. "Blessed be the God and Father of our Lord Jesus Christ, the Father of mercies and God of all comfort, who comforts us in all our tribulation, that we may be able to comfort those who are in any trouble, with the comfort with which we ourselves are comforted by God. For as the sufferings of Christ abound in us, so our consolation also abounds through Christ. Now if we are afflicted, it is for your consolation and salvation, which is effective for enduring the same sufferings which we also suffer. Or if we are comforted, it is for your consolation and salvation. And our hope for you is steadfast, because we know that as you are partakers of the sufferings, so also you will partake of the consolation."

Faith had read those scriptures numerous times in her life, but she'd never had them explained like they were that evening. The teacher pointed out that Christians could comfort others because God had comforted them. If God had never given comfort to His people, they wouldn't know how to give it themselves. That meant that even though no one wanted to go through bad things, at least when they had to, good could come of it. The people who had been consoled through the bad could offer the same support to others suffering similar circumstances.

It was a new way for her to look at good coming from affliction.

She pointed that out to Sam as they headed back to the hotel after services. "Do you believe everything they said at church tonight?"

Sam thought for a moment before he answered. "I don't know. I don't believe God lets bad things happen to us just so that good can come from them. But we do live in a sinful world, Faith. Other people make bad decisions, and their decisions have consequences that sometimes can affect our lives. I believe God can work good from that. And sometimes bad things just happen because this life is not perfect. We'll only live in a perfect place when we get to Heaven. Until then, we have to deal with things happening that we don't always want to happen."

"I'm struggling with finding any good that could come out of us losing Moira." Faith stared out the elevator window.

"Well, for one thing, we're not very far removed from it yet." Sam pulled her to his side as they walked down the hall to their room. "So, there's no telling what kinds of great things are in store for us."

Faith nodded.

"And for another thing, it might not even be something that happens to us that is good. It might be something that we can be to someone else because we've been through this experience. Just like they were talking about in class tonight. Maybe God can use us in other ways now than He could before because we've suffered the loss of a child—He gave up His child for all of us, but we never really knew the pain that it would be to know the loss of a child until now. I'm not saying that God wanted us to feel that pain. But I am saying that now we're better equipped to help others who go through this, too. To comfort them like we've been comforted. And who knows who all you reach through your blog ... someone might be out there who sees your faith through this and how you continue to trust in God to see you through. It's not easy, but you're sticking with it anyway. You might be touching all sorts of people out there in the blogosphere that you may never even know about."

Faith sat on the edge of the bed. "I never really thought about that."

"I think a lot of the people who have tried to use that Romans verse in the past have used it in the wrong way—or not expressed themselves like they meant to. But that's the way I feel about it." Sam plopped down next to her.

"I decided several years ago that I needed to make a decision—to love and trust God to get me through all of this because He will make it right in the end and to quit getting mad at Him when something else didn't work to bring about the results we had wanted. If I can't trust Him, I can't blame Him either. There's no either/or. God doesn't change who He is just because my situation changes. I won't go back on that decision now." Faith pulled her knees to her chest. "God loves me no matter what, so why shouldn't I reciprocate?"

"Makes sense to me." Sam nodded.

"I wish that made it easier to deal with the pain." Her voice came out squeaky.

"I think it is making it easier. Imagine how much harder it would be if we didn't have our faith and our church family. How horrible it would be to not know if your child was in Heaven, waiting on you to get there someday, too."

"I'm so glad I married you." She wrapped her arms around his waist and leaned her head on his shoulder.

"The feeling's mutual." He pressed a kiss to her hair.

"Now I wish I could find a way to help Hope through her rough spot, too." Faith buried her head into him a little more.

"You're such a fixer." He gave her a smile to show he was teasing. "But I think this time she's going to have to work it out on her own."

CHAPTER 24

HOPE

"You're not driving, are you?" Joe asked on Friday. "That's like a ten- or twelve-hour drive!"

Hope shook her head. "No. I'm flying. I found some fairly reasonable tickets, and the school has agreed to pay at least part of my travel expenses since it's such late notice and everything."

She had an interview set up for this coming Monday at a school back in Mississippi. She had called them as soon as she had seen the posting Tuesday and gotten the voice mail from them Wednesday, and they had worked it all out on Thursday. She would fly to Memphis on Saturday, get picked up by Cassidy, ride to Oxford, hang out the rest of the weekend, have the interview Monday morning, and fly back Monday afternoon. It was going to be a crazy trip, but it was the first time she actually felt like things were going her way. When the school got her résumé, they thought it was perfect for what they needed, and they were willing to start her salary at the fifth-year teacher level instead of the third since she had her master's degree.

"Faith dropping you at the airport?" Joe asked.

"Yes. She got back last night. I'll fly out early Saturday. Be back late Monday."

Joe was silent as he watched the boys chase each other all over the playground equipment. Music floated over from a pavilion close by where another group was playing a game of Freeze Dance. Hope enjoyed a brief moment of breeze as it cooled her neck and forehead and lifted some hairs that had fallen out of her braid.

"We'll miss you Monday." He walked over to the other side of the slides. She could tell he was upset about something but wasn't sure what. After all, he was headed to another country after this summer. Why should she try to stick to this area if he wasn't going to be here anyway? She shook it off and got through the rest of the day so she could go home and start packing for her trip the next day.

∽

"CALL ME IF ANYTHING CHANGES." Faith pulled up to the door of the airport the next day. "Let me know you got there safely and everything."

"Sure." Hope shouldered her carry-on and her purse and leaned back into the car for just a moment. "Thanks for the ride. Pray hard!"

"I haven't stopped." Faith waved before pulling away from the curb.

Austin wasn't the biggest airport Hope had been to, but it was large enough that she paused inside the doors to gather her bearings. She joined the line to go through security since she had printed out her boarding pass the night before and was not going to check her bags. She wanted everything to be perfect on this trip. Slowly, they inched forward until it was her turn.

Hope showed her boarding pass and driver's license. When she got the nod from the security guard, she walked through the metal detector and was glad when nothing set it off. She picked up her bags and shoes and continued to the left until she found the correct gate. This early on a Saturday morning, the terminals were fairly quiet. She sat in one of the leather chairs and stored her suitcase between her legs while she dug a book out of her purse. Maybe if she focused on the story, she could quit thinking about other things ... namely Joe.

The screen said her flight was on time. She had just under an hour to wait until it was time to go. She settled in and tried to fight her impatience, but her feet tapped erratically as the minutes slowly ticked by. Hope couldn't wait to hug Cassidy's neck and see her friends in Mississippi. The only thing that put a damper on this trip was Joe's reaction when she told him yesterday. She tried to let that roll off her mind, but it lingered in the background as in vain she attempted to focus on the novel in her hands.

Several hours later, the plane touched down on the other side of the Mississippi river. Hope had watched out the window for it from the moment the plane had reached cruising altitude despite knowing she had an hour or so of Texas and all of Louisiana to cross before she could see the beautiful landmark. It glistened below, curving its way down to the gulf.

"Almost home."

The Memphis airport was small, but she still almost missed where she was supposed to go when she looked down for a moment to check a text from Cassidy. She looked back up just in time to see the sign pointing down to Baggage. She took a quick step onto the escalator and searched the crowd for her roommate's face. It was hard to miss that red hair and the poster board Cassidy had decorated in large letters to welcome Hope home.

Cassidy squealed with delight as she wrapped her arms around Hope. "Girl, you are so tan!"

Hope looked down at her arms and smiled. "I freckle well, anyway."

On the ride down to Oxford, Cassidy filled Hope in on how her summer had gone with her cousin Amy as a roommate. "I love my cousin, but she's not you. I don't think I have to say anything else."

"Faith isn't you, either." Hope laughed. "But it really hasn't been as bad as I thought it would be."

"That sounds very mature of you." Cassidy's voice dripped with sarcasm.

"I guess I've had to do some maturing this summer. It's not every summer you start thinking you're going to be an aunt and end without that hope."

Cassidy reached over and squeezed Hope's hand.

"Faith and I are getting along a lot better, actually." Hope studied a scrape on the back of one of her hands, probably obtained from playing at camp. "I guess it was a sort of wakeup call when I discovered she hadn't let me in on any of their infertility struggles the last few years. I knew our relationship wasn't great, but I hadn't realized it was so bad we couldn't tell each other important things."

"I'm glad you're closer with your sister now." Cassidy drummed the steering wheel in time with the beat of the song playing on the radio. "But I'm also so, so glad you're back ... even if it's only for a few days."

"Me, too. I missed having you around to hash things out with. Email and texts just aren't the same."

"Speaking of hashing things out ... thought about Kyle any while you were away?" Cassidy wiggled her eyebrows. "I saw him the other day, and he asked about you."

Hope gave a sheepish grin. "Not at all, actually."

"You're blushing!" Cassidy exclaimed as she took the exit back to the apartment. "You met someone, didn't you? You fell in love with a cowboy!"

"He's not a cowboy." Hope thought about the dark Latino guy she had spent almost every day of the summer with. "But, yes. I met someone."

"And?"

"His name is Joe and he's a co-counselor at camp and he goes to church with Faith and Sam." Hope said it all in a rush.

"And?" Cassidy prompted again.

"And he's very sweet and handsome and fun and smart and such a good Christian." Hope couldn't keep her voice from sounding a bit sad.

"Is he dating someone else?" Cassidy asked.

"No." Hope refused to give any further explanation.

"Hope, what's wrong? You're not keeping yourself from this really great guy just because he lives in Texas, are you? I thought you were even considering moving there this fall if you could find a job."

"Cass, it's more complicated than that."

Cassidy didn't push any further as she pulled into the parking lot. "Since Amy is still here, you're bunking with me."

"That's fine." Hope gave a smile. "We used to do that on weekends when we were in school, too. I think I can still manage sleeping in the same room with you, even if you do snore."

"Hey." Cassidy gave Hope a playful push on the arm.

It was great to be back in Mississippi with its rolling hills and tall trees. Hope took a deep breath of the humid July air before she followed her roommate into the apartment. It was mostly the same as she remembered, except instead of her things scattered over half the dining table, Cassidy's cousin's possessions had taken over.

"Thought we could go to that burger place you like so much." Cassidy leaned against the door frame as Hope stashed her things in Cassidy's bedroom.

"Sounds good." Hope nodded.

The night was spent reminiscing and laughing. Hope shared funny stories about the kids at camp, little anecdotes they had said or silly antics they did. She tried to avoid the topic of Joe, but he kept popping into her thoughts and therefore into her conversation. It seemed he was a major part of everything she had done this summer. Her breath caught in her throat at the thought she might never see him again after August.

Cassidy didn't snore that night, but Hope still couldn't find a way to fall asleep. She lay on her side on her half of Cassidy's bed and stared at the lights coming in the window through the cracks in the blind. She had forgotten how noisy apartment life was after living in her sister's quiet neighborhood for a month and a half.

Her hair refused to cooperate the next morning, no matter what she did to it. She finally pulled it into a braid and decided to pretend like frizzles weren't escaping from it every second. Maybe she didn't like the humidity after all, even if it was better for her skin. She would never admit that to Faith, though.

Worship services and Bible class were just as great as they had always been but Hope missed Joe. He always had a great comment or thought to add to the Bible lesson. And he had gotten to where he sat close enough to Hope that she could usually hear his bass voice as he dipped down to the low notes. She continued to be amazed at how every now and then his voice literally vibrated the pew.

"Missing Joe?" Cassidy interrupted her thoughts as they walked around a shopping center that afternoon.

Hope glanced at her friend. She waivered only a moment before deciding to admit what was troubling her. "Yes. And it doesn't matter because there's no hope for this relationship to go anywhere. He's going to Honduras this fall to be a missionary."

"That's awesome." Cassidy pointed to an empty bench and they sat down.

"It is." Hope picked a leaf up and twisted it around in her fingers.

"But?"

"But he's going to be in another country. I'm trying to find a teaching job here. Where does that leave us? I can't imagine a long-distance thing would be any good. They don't even always have good internet service down there. It just wouldn't work." Hope shook her head.

Cassidy pulled her into a side hug. "We need ice cream."

Hope laughed. "I missed you so much."

∼

THE NEXT MORNING, Hope was up hours before her alarm. She had tossed and turned again the night before, trying to find sleep but instead worrying about this job interview—and about Joe. She snuck out of the bedroom and turned on the lamp by the couch so she could do her Bible reading. It was something Joe had challenged her to do each morning towards the beginning of the summer. She had gotten several days behind and figured this was as good a time as any to catch up.

She opened her Bible to Romans 5, where she had left off. Around verse 3, she could almost hear Joe's voice reading the words to her. "And not only that, but we also glory in tribulations, knowing that tribulation produces perseverance; and perseverance, character; and character, hope. Now hope does not disappoint, because the love of God has been poured out in our hearts by the Holy Spirit who was given to us."

I'm trying, God. I'm trying to hope. It's just so hard. I thought having this job interview would help, but now I seem to have even more doubts and insecurities than I did before.

She got ready with plenty of time to get to her interview, caught the bus that stopped closest to the school, and headed out to find a job. The campus was clean enough, with windows looking out onto a spacious lawn. Several teenagers hung out on benches in front of the building and Hope wondered if they were summer school students or athletes—there weren't many other reasons a teenager would be at a school during the summer. She entered the double doors and followed the signs to the office.

The principal, Ms. Tinsley, was nice enough. She asked all the questions Hope had prepared for. Ms. Tinsley explained the positions they were looking to fill, as well as the other activities teachers were expected to participate in at this school. She explained some of their policies on discipline and grades. Then, she took Hope on a tour of the campus and asked if she had any questions of her own.

"I can't think of any right now." Hope smoothed her hands over her skirt, trying not to fidget.

"We've got a couple more applicants set up with interviews for later this week, so we'll touch base with you to let you know our decision by Friday." Ms. Tinsley shook Hope's hand one more time. She handed Hope a reimbursement check for half of her travel expenses, and then the interview was over.

Hope had no idea how it had gone. She thought she had answered everything right, but looking back on it, she wondered if she couldn't have stated some things more succinctly or clearer. She passed another girl a little older than she was as she left the office. The girl was also dressed for an interview, and Hope wondered if she was applying for the same position. She watched through the window for a minute to see Ms. Tinsley welcome the girl in the same way she had greeted Hope just an hour before.

Hope shook her head and walked back outside into the late morning heat. She caught the bus back to Cassidy's apartment, changed into something more comfortable, and waited for her friend to get home so she could start her journey back. She double- and triple-checked her bags before Cassidy rushed through the doors.

"Sorry I'm late. I'll get you there on time!"

"You're not that late, and we had figured extra time just in case anyway, so we're good." Hope followed her roommate's lead and quickly got into the car to head north.

"How did it go?" Cassidy switched lanes to pass a slower truck.

"I have no idea." Hope picked at a rough spot on her jeans. "I feel so unqualified and desperate when I go to these things."

"If you can't believe you're a good teacher, how can you convince the schools that you are?" Cassidy cut her a glance.

Hope sighed. "I don't know."

"What happened to my friend who used to be cheerful and happy and fun to hang out with?"

"Sorry. Just worried." Hope watched the scenery fly by outside the car window. She loved this area, but she was going to be flying back to Texas this afternoon and back at camp tomorrow. After that, she had no idea.

On the way here, she had considered herself as coming home. So, why did it feel even more that way now that she was headed back to the state she previously swore she never wanted to live in? Was it the state itself? The friendly people? One person in particular?

CHAPTER 25

FAITH

Faith stared at the blank screen in front of her. She saw her blog in a whole new light since her talk with Sam several nights before in San Antonio. God had blessed her a million times over when He let her marry that man. She said a quiet prayer of thanksgiving before she reopened the first post she had ever put on this website.

As she skimmed through her entries from the last three years, she noticed for the first time how visible her growth was. When she had started her blog, they had been in the beginnings of the fertility treatment process. She had had no idea that she would go three more years without conceiving. Or that she would get pregnant and then lose the baby.

Her early posts were about the ups and downs of waiting through another cycle while her body decided whether or not it would give in to the pills and hormones she was subjecting it to. Month after month, she had posted, "Negative again."

When she got to the dark period of just a few years ago, she read those posts more thoroughly. She was almost ashamed of how little faith she had held onto during those months. She had written about being depressed, jealous of other people as they had their own children, tired of the struggle each month to keep her chin up as she let Sam stab her in the bottom with another shot of hormones.

Several friends had commented on her blog through that time that they were worried about her and wished she would go see a psychiatrist. She probably had suffered from clinical depression during that stretch, but she would never have admitted it. And she had no desire to go see another doctor on top of the ones she was already seeing several times a month.

She skimmed through the "breakthrough" post, the one where she had written about her epiphany.

I was thinking today, and I realized something. I'm not ready to go to Heaven. Have you ever thought about that? What if Jesus came back today? Would you be ready, excited, happy to see Him? I know I want to see Him, and I want to go to Heaven. But I have let my desire to be a mommy take that away from me. Instead of focusing on God and how I can serve Him through this time of my life, I'm bemoaning how He is not answering my prayers the way I want Him to. I find myself telling Him that His timing is not perfect. Sounds rather petty, doesn't it?

Faith soaked up the words she had written. That was the day she had begun to rethink their life. She had talked with Sam about it and told him what she had figured out. He had agreed that it did sometimes seem like their infertility got in the way of being Christians.

With tears and a very fervent prayer that night, both of them had decided to quit trying to get pregnant and just take a break to get their priorities back in order. That had been in January, just seven months before. Once they quit actively trying to conceive, it had taken them less than four months to get pregnant. Her doctor had been impressed.

Reading through the few posts she had managed to pen the last month, Faith thought she could detect a little bit of the depression that she had suffered from almost two years before. But it had not been the whole theme. Her blog rang with Bible verses that were full of comfort, with promises of God's faithfulness and love. She had recorded thoughts on the child she would never meet this side of Heaven, but the post had been more hopeful than sad.

She could see her growth. She hoped anyone who stumbled across her site could also see it. And that it would help them.

She opened a new page and thought for a moment before titling it, "A Dawning."

As you all know, this summer has been ... well, not the best. It started out great. I was pregnant at last and was enjoying even the little discomforts that come with it because it meant I was finally going to get to be a mommy. Then, the end of June brought about a change, and suddenly, all my plans and hopes and dreams went down a drain ... almost literally.

My child was miscarried at only ten and a half weeks. It was still too early to know the gender, but we decided it was a girl, and we named her Moira. And, if you have been reading my recent posts, you can see that I did not come through this completely unscathed.

This last week, my husband and I took a few days to go to San Antonio and celebrate our seventh anniversary. While we were there seeing the sights, we also got to have deep conversations and know how the other was honestly doing since the miscarriage. I am blessed beyond measure with the man I married seven years ago. He is a spiritual leader in my life that I could never have dreamed of.

As I was bemoaning the fact that it wasn't fair that God had taken away our child and wondering what good could come of it, he calmly took my hands and pointed out that we had no idea what would happen because of this. I agree with him that God would never want us to hurt this way, though. After all, God lost His son for a while, too. He knows how it feels.

Sam also pointed out that our situation might touch people who we may never meet. I know more than my friends read my blog. Maybe one of you reading this now is going through something similar and just typed in 'infertility' and found your way to my site. If so, I pray that God will use my hurts and healings as I post them on here to share with you and that they will benefit you in some way as you continue your journey towards motherhood, too.

In other words, more than ever, I want to make this blog a testament of my faith in God. I may not always think His timing is perfect, but I know in my heart that it is. And I know that He will never change or waver. He is the same today as He was yesterday and as He will be forever. I am the only one in this relationship changing. And I pray He will change me for the better.

As always, say a prayer for us as we continue to desire to be parents. And say a prayer for all the other couples the world over as there are many out there going through similar pain. And thank God that we can have a relationship with Him that will comfort and guide us in this process.

Thanks for reading my blog. I hope it blesses you in some way!

Faith clicked on the "post" button, and her newest piece went live. She had uploaded pictures earlier in the week of the scrapbook album she had made to commemorate her short pregnancy. There were also some new photos she and Sam had taken down in San Antonio.

She didn't want her site to be only about the heartache and suffering that came with infertility. She wanted it to be a complete picture of her life. And, all in all, she was very blessed.

As she admitted that to herself, she also admitted that her sister was one of the blessings. She wasn't sure what to do with that though. After the job interview in Mississippi, Hope had shut herself away more than ever. Faith had thought they were getting over that, but something had changed lately, and Faith couldn't put her finger on what it was.

She saw Joe watching Hope every time she was in the same room with both of them. She knew something was going on there, but she didn't know how it would work out. "God, it's in your hands, but please help them figure something out. They both look so miserable," she prayed.

CHAPTER 26

HOPE

*I*t didn't surprise Hope to find Joe waiting for her at the bottom of the escalators instead of Faith. After all, he had been on her mind all weekend, and she liked to fancy that maybe she had been on his, too. He pulled her into more of a hug than she was expecting, but she couldn't complain about being right where she wanted to be.

"How did it go?" He carried her bag as they walked to where he had parked his Jeep.

"Not completely sure." She shifted her purse strap.

He just nodded as he stored her things in the backseat. "We missed you at camp today."

"It probably would have been more enjoyable than going through an interview." She was not going to be hurt by the fact that he said "we" instead of "I."

"Up for some dinner? I thought it would be fun to show you some things in Austin since we're down here anyway."

"Sure." She watched the scenery out the window. Sunflowers filled in the medians with bright yellow faces. They weren't giant ones like she was used to, but she had to admit they were pretty.

Joe wove through downtown traffic like it didn't even exist

despite the fact that it was rush hour. They passed the huge, pink Texas State Capitol building and then turned south. He stopped at a cluster of food trucks, complete with picnic tables and shade trees.

"I know it's not fancy, but they really do have some of the best burritos in town." He pointed through the window.

Talk stayed light, Joe filling her in on what she had missed that day with the first-grade boys. She answered his questions about her flight and her roommate. It was late enough in the day that shadows crept across their picnic table and the sky was beginning to turn rosy.

Joe grabbed her hand and pulled her back to the car. "Come on. We have just enough time."

"Just enough time for what?" She had to almost run to keep up with his long legs.

"You'll see."

They were soon parked again and walking down a hill to a riverside park. A walking track ran the length of the water, and families gathered at the edge or on the sidewalks of the bridge overhead. Hope wrinkled her nose at the smell but continued to let herself be dragged along by Joe. He finally settled on a rock just large enough for two people to sit on, and he tugged her down beside him.

"There's a lot of people down here." She glanced around again.

"They're all waiting for the show." Joe gave a half-grin.

"The show?"

"You'll see." He nodded toward the river.

They sat quietly for a few moments before he turned to her and took both of her hands in his. She studied his deep brown eyes as she waited for whatever he was about to say. Instead, he sighed and faced the water once more.

"What's wrong, Joe?" she asked.

"Everything." His shoulders slumped.

"That doesn't sound like you."

"No. It sort of sounds more like what you've been saying all summer." He gave a halfhearted chuckle.

Hope bit back a smart-alecky remark. "Is that what you meant when you said I don't live up to my name?"

He looked at her with confusion written all over his face.

"The other day when it rained ..." She tilted her head. "I had found out about you being named Josiah, and you mentioned something about the fact that Faith and I were both named for the things we seem to struggle with the most."

"I guess I didn't even realize you heard me." He nodded. "But yes, sort of."

She watched a couple boats as they lazily made their way out to the middle of the river, then stopped just under the bridge. Even more people lined the top of the bridge, staring east and leaning over the railing. Several vendors pushed ice cream carts or hawked glow sticks.

"So, I struggle with hope." She said it as a statement. But it was also, in part, a question to make sure she understood exactly what he was saying. And maybe a little bit of an accusation.

"Look, I didn't mean it as an insult." Joe turned to her again. "I pointed it out because I worry about you. I know I haven't known you for very long, but sometimes it feels like I've known you forever. I can't imagine a day without you. Trust me, these last few days have been crazy. But you can't seem to see that your life is so great. You have a family who loves you so much that they're willing to bend over backwards to help you overcome any obstacle in your life. You got that interview back in Oxford as soon as you called, so you must be a good teacher. You have friends who care enough about you that they'll drive to the airport to pick you up."

"I know all of that." Hope spread her hands.

"Then why can you only focus on the bad stuff? You've been carrying a rain cloud over your head all summer." Joe held his hand just over her hair. "I ask you how an interview went, and you act like you're not even good enough to have considered going in the first place. I just hate seeing such a beautiful, talented, smart woman not see how great she is."

Hope swallowed all the compliments he had just paid her in a roundabout way. "What do you expect? I moved out here like that, but then I discovered camp wasn't as bad as I had thought it would be. But I met this guy who seems to like me, and I don't have a way of staying with even if we do ever get together. Because you're going to—"

"Honduras." He finished her statement. "As you keep reminding me."

The noise of the crowd around them changed, and they both looked toward the river. The sun was about as low in the west as it could get without sinking beneath the horizon. It left just enough light for her to make out millions of small fluttering shapes flowing out from underneath the bridge.

"Are those—?"

"Bats." He nodded.

A shiver crept up her back. While the idea of seeing that many bats at once was a bit eerie, it was also really cool. They seemed to form a stream that undulated through the air, heading east. She watched for several minutes, and they continued to fly out until she couldn't imagine how they had all fit under there.

"They fly out every evening at sunset and head up river to do their hunting. Then, they all make their way back by dawn and return to the bridge to sleep away the day. Millions and millions of Mexican free-tailed bats. I love coming down here and watching them, but I don't get to do it very often." Joe's eyes stayed glued to the sight.

Even after it was completely night, the bats still trickled out from under the bridge. Joe finally stood up and helped her to her feet.

"You've had a long day, and camp is early tomorrow. Better get you back to the McCreary house."

"We didn't finish our talk." She tried to make out his facial expression in the growing dark.

"No. I thought you had ended it." His body remained stiffly beside her, as if he were forcing himself to not reach out.

"Joe, I want a chance at us. I really like you." Hope tentatively touched his arm. "I just can't do long-distance."

"The guy who is coming back stateside isn't coming back right away. I was going down in September just so he could start showing me the ropes. We've got time." Joe's voice still sounded uncertain.

"And then what?"

Joe jumped down off the rock. "Does everything have to be settled right this very moment?"

"No." Hope shook her head, resisting the urge to scream in frustration. "But it would be nice to know that I'm not going to end up broken-hearted when you head south."

Joe didn't say anything for a moment. She could barely make out what his face looked like by the light of the streetlamps now that he was back down on the path. He appeared to be arguing with himself.

"What, Joe?" she asked.

He let out a breath. "My mother, she told me not to do this yet. She said you weren't ready."

"Ready for what?" Hope narrowed her eyes.

"What's stopping you from coming south with me?" He asked it quickly, as if he were afraid if he said it too slowly, he wouldn't say it at all.

Going with him?

"Joe?"

"Come to Honduras with me. You don't have a job lined up yet. There's nothing to keep you here or in Mississippi right now. Why not?"

Why not? Wait! Go with him?

"I can't go with you. We're not married. We're not even dating!" Why did it seem like this talk had gone from crazy to completely insane? "Two single people shouldn't run off to a foreign country together."

"We can change that."

Change that? "Was that a proposal?" She was now thoroughly confused by this whole conversation.

"Yes? No." He ran a hand through his hair. "Maybe? None of this is going how I thought it would. I've been thinking all day about how to say exactly what I wanted to say, and now the words are nowhere to be found."

She waited for him to go on. What else could she do? It definitely wasn't any kind of proposal she had dreamed about. Nor what she had expected to happen this evening.

He let out a breath. "Hope, you know me, right?"

"Well, I thought I was getting to know you."

"We've worked together almost every day for the last two months. You've seen me angry and happy. You've seen me at church and eaten with my mother and me. I know you. And I know your sister and her husband, so I can get a sense of what your family is like. I've even met your parents a couple times when they visited.

"Maybe it's not perfect, but I know that while you were gone this weekend I kept looking for you." Joe swung their clasped hands back and forth between them as he continued to talk. "I would have taken you out on Saturday, and enjoyed hearing your comments in Bible class Sunday, and loved having you working with me at camp today. I kept thinking about things I wanted to share with you, or jokes you would have found funny. Please tell me you feel at least a little bit the same way about me."

Hope chewed on her bottom lip for a moment. Was she actually going to admit this? "Cassidy told me that all I talked about all weekend was you. I didn't realize it when I was doing it, but evidently, you've become a huge part of my life this summer."

"Yeah?"

"Yeah," she whispered.

People walked by them, headed home after the amazing bat show. Joe didn't seem to notice. He kept his gaze fixed on her as the moonlight played with his expressions.

"I don't have to make any decisions tonight, do I?" Hope finally broke their silence.

"No." Joe ducked his head for a moment. "But I know that it will be a lot easier to get on that plane in September if you're on it with me."

Hope shook her head. "I still don't know about this. I've never even thought of doing missionary work." Did that sound bad? Weren't all Christians meant to be missionaries in one form or another? She stopped and looked at him with wide eyes. "Joe, I can't speak a lick of Spanish!"

He laughed. "So, I'll teach you. You'll be fine."

"No, seriously. I can't even remember how to count all the way to ten. My high school Spanish is gone."

"Hope, there you go looking for the bad instead of the good again." He brushed a hair back from her face and cupped her cheek in his hand.

Several cat calls were thrown their way, and Hope realized just how public a show they had been putting on. "We were supposed to be going, weren't we?"

He lingered another moment before he nodded. "Okay. Let's get you to bed."

"I don't even have a passport." Her mind raced faster than his Jeep did as they headed north on I-35.

"That's something that can be fixed." He was always so matter-of-fact. Did nothing faze him?

"What if we couldn't get it in time?" Hope asked.

He glanced at her. "We're not on a set schedule. The team will be happy to have us whenever we can get down there."

He had already started talking about it like she was for sure going. Part of her loved that. It was so easy to let herself believe that he was right and that everything could be perfect if they would just take the leap. She wouldn't have to be away from him.

The more reasonable side of her was arguing madly, trying to bring her back to earth. There was no way they could work out all these details in less than two months. But she didn't have a job lined up yet in Mississippi ... or Texas. And it had to be better than staying in Texas or moving back in with her parents, right?

Her phone jingled, and she checked the text. "Did you make it safely?"

"Who is it?" Joe asked.

"Cassidy. She just wanted to make sure I was safely here."

Hope quickly typed a reply. "Safe. Joe picked me up. Call you later."

Hope leaned back against the beat-up leather seat and stared at Joe's profile. Could he end up being the person she saw next to her every day for the rest of her life? After several years of dating someone who had no clue what he wanted to do with his life, it seemed like she had shifted to the other end of the pendulum swing. Joe was so certain of everything, like he had an inner voice inside him telling him it was going to work out. It was a little bit disconcerting.

"Whatcha thinkin'?" He caught her staring at him.

"About how you never seem to doubt that everything will be fine." She pointed between the two of them. "You're like my opposite, I guess. If you really do think that I'm all moping and bemoaning."

"Hey! Opposites attract." He reached over and gave her hand a squeeze.

"Joe, do you really think it could work?" She let out a sigh.

"It will if we make it work." He signaled to get off at their exit. "God doesn't give us opportunities and then make us face any problems that come with them alone. He's always with us and will help us through whatever struggles may be waiting for us on the other side of a decision. I don't believe that He's willing us to choose one way or another. That sounds too much like taking away our free will. But He will use us and bless us in more ways than we can imagine as long as we choose a path that follows Him."

"That was a lot deeper than I was expecting."

"I just had a feeling the question was about more than just you and me getting together, but about life in general. Will everything always be perfect and go the way we want it to? No. God never promises us that. But He does promise a rainbow after the rain. And He does promise an eternal reward with Him in Heaven. What more could you ask for?"

Hope thought about that as they entered Faith's neighborhood. Joe meandered down the sleepy streets, as if he wanted to make the evening last as long as he possibly could. She didn't mind. It meant that much longer she could sit beside him, her hand in his. He finally pulled into the driveway and cut the engine and lights.

The porch light was on, but the house looked dark otherwise. "Guess they went to bed already."

"It is a bit later than I meant to keep you out." Joe gave a sheepish grin.

"It was worth it." She bit back a moan as he gently pulled his hand away from hers.

"I hope you still feel the same first thing in the morning."

"You're not bringing me coffee?" She laughed.

He got out and came around to open her door. Such a gentleman, he also got her luggage out and walked her up to the front stoop. She turned to take her bags only to find him inches from her. She looked up into his eyes, and her breath caught in her throat. He leaned forward and kissed her, gentle and slow. This time, she didn't pull away.

"I'm not going to force you to do anything you don't want to, Hope." His whisper caressed her cheek. "But I've grown to care for you very deeply this summer. I can't imagine leaving you at the end of it."

After what seemed like an eternal moment, he pressed one last kiss to her forehead and stepped back. She unlocked the door and let herself in to the quiet house. She heard him pull out and watched as the lights flew across the living room as he turned to go down the street toward his house. Was this what Maria was talking about on the Fourth of July when she had said their ways would part at the end of the summer only if she let them? How was she supposed to make a decision like this with so little time?

CHAPTER 27

FAITH

"You couldn't sleep either?" Hope interrupted Faith's quiet solitude several nights later.

"No." Faith shifted her position on the sofa, her computer in her lap and a mug of cocoa in her hands. "Too much on my mind, I guess."

"Mind if I join you?"

"There's more hot chocolate." Faith moved to fix some, but Hope waved her back.

"I know where it is."

Faith listened to the sounds of her sister in the kitchen. At the beginning of the summer, she'd thought she would never get used to having Hope here. Now it was strange to think of her leaving in the next couple of weeks. She pulled her legs up closer and moved the laptop to the floor beside her as Hope returned to the living room and sat at the other end of the couch with her own mug.

"I never got a chance to apologize for letting Joe surprise you like that on Monday." Faith cut a glance at her sister over the rim of her cup. "But I guess you've forgiven him since you two were sitting pretty close at church last night."

Hope gave a guilty look. "I probably should have said something earlier ..."

"You finally gave in?" Faith picked a marshmallow from the warm liquid.

"He asked me to go to Honduras with him."

Faith's breath caught. Hope hadn't looked so happy all summer. But it wasn't perfect happiness. She also appeared a bit lost.

"I'm guessing you're considering it."

"I don't want to think about not seeing him every day." Hope crossed her legs under her. "We've gotten really close this summer. I mean, we've been together pretty much every day for the last seven weeks. I tried to fight it, but I just couldn't. He's so great. How was I supposed to not fall in love with that?"

Faith laughed. "He is great. But it's a huge decision. I mean, we're talking about you moving to a whole other country."

"I know." Hope's voice came out a little whiny. "And that's a huge step for me. I've never been out of the country. I've never been out of the southeastern United States, really. I don't even own a passport. And I don't speak Spanish. This is ridiculous. Why am I even considering it?"

"Because it's Joe." Faith set her mug aside.

"Joe." Hope repeated the name in a breathy voice, a dreamy expression on her face.

"Where would you stay? Would one of the other families on the team have a room for you?"

"That's the other part. When he said he was hoping I would go with him, I think it was sort of a proposal."

"A marriage proposal?" Faith sat up straighter.

"Sort of." Hope wrinkled her nose.

"How can it be 'sort of' a marriage proposal?" Faith leaned forward.

"Well, he didn't actually ask me in so many words to marry him, but when I asked if it was a proposal, he admitted he didn't want to spend the rest of his life without me."

Faith shook her head. "I'm going to skin that boy. He didn't even do it right. What kind of a proposal is that?"

Hope giggled as Faith continued to fuss over the way Joe had asked. Faith stopped talking and started laughing, too. She leaned back against the arm of the couch again.

Hope sighed. "My brain is telling me I'm crazy to even be thinking about any of this. It's too much all at once. To go from thinking I was going to move back in with Cassidy and teach again this fall, to starting to think that maybe it would be really cool to be a missionary in Honduras with Joe. How did I even get here?"

"What is your heart telling you?"

"That I want to be with Joe even if it means having to learn a new language in a month and a half." Hope threw her hands in the air.

"Wow. I hadn't even thought about that." Faith shook her head. "I can't remember much of high school Spanish, can you?"

"Just a few of the numbers, *no*, and that *manzana* is *apple*."

"Why on earth do you remember the word for *apple*?" Faith asked.

"Our teacher's name was Mr. Apple. We translated it." Hope shrugged.

"As long as they grow apples down there, you won't starve anyway."

They laughed again. It was a silly idea covering up all the little things that were real problems that could hinder this plan from actually happening. Faith thought for several moments about it all, still a little shocked that one of her best friends had fallen in love with her sister.

"Remember when we used to sneak out of bed late at night and play dolls by the light of the nightlight?" Hope traced the swirly pattern of the couch cushion.

Faith smiled at the memory. "I would always make you be the boy doll."

"And you would always take Moira Angela as your own."

Faith nodded.

"Sitting up here in the dark sort of reminds me of that. Do you think Mom ever knew?" Hope asked.

Faith snorted. "Knowing her, she probably did."

Hope grinned in return. "Probably. One day we'll be like that, too. When we have kids."

"*If* we have kids." Faith couldn't hold the correction back.

Hope shook her head. "Nope. When."

Faith cocked an eyebrow.

"Joe's been helping me figure some things out." Hope propped her elbows on her knees. "We're both named after really great biblical principles, both of which you need to be a strong Christian. But you've struggled with the faith part. And I'm still struggling with keeping hold of the hope. It's like Mom named us after what she knew would be hardest for us. But in the end, it's just like the verse says."

"The greatest of these is love." They quoted the rest of the verse together.

"Without the love of God, we couldn't have faith *or* hope. We just have to remember how much God loves us so that we can hold on to our faith and our hope." Hope rolled her eyes. "That's super simplistic, but I think you get the basic idea."

"Joe's been good for you." Faith nudged Hope with her toe.

"I hate to admit it, but I think this whole summer has been good for me." Hope ducked her head. "Having to get out of my comfort zone, having to face things I thought I would hate, having to deal with living under someone else's rules instead of my own again. None of it was easy. But there were a lot of good things, too."

"Like Joe." Faith smirked.

"Like Joe." Hope beamed. "And figuring out that maybe there's something else I could do besides be a teacher. I never considered going into the mission field before, but I've been reading the blog the team has been keeping about their work down there, and I'm really starting to get excited about it."

"You know what all this means, don't you?" Faith laughed.

"What?"

"Mom was right." Faith covered her mouth as soon as the words had escaped.

Hope buried her head in a throw pillow for a moment. "Let's make a pact to never tell her that."

"You girls are awful giggly out here." Sam leaned against the doorway.

Faith and Hope both started. Neither one had heard him coming down the hallway. Then, they exchanged a glance with each other and burst into laughter again.

"Sorry, honey. We'll try to keep it down." Faith chewed on her bottom lip to keep the mirth at bay long enough to apologize.

He shook his head and shuffled back the way he'd come.

"He's trying to get back into a school schedule again since it's only a few weeks away." Faith pointed toward the calendar over the desk. "Therefore, he's not supposed to stay up late at night any more this summer unless it's on a weekend. Guess I'm not as motivated as he is to get back on a normal schedule again."

"I know it's going to be hard to get up and go to camp again in the morning." Hope yawned. "But my mind was going so many different directions, I couldn't even focus enough to go to sleep."

"I understand." Faith nodded.

They sat in the quiet for a few moments, leaving each other to her own thoughts. The clock ticked across the room. Cicadas sang their songs outside the window. A car drove by, its lights shining across the room and then disappearing again. Faith finished off her mug of cocoa.

"Faith?" Hope broke the silence.

"Hmm?"

"Do you think it's my fault you lost the baby?"

Faith's heart clenched. It wasn't the question she was expecting to come after what they had been talking about this night. Or ever. She scooted to where she could wrap Hope up in a hug.

"No, Hopey. I don't think it was your fault. It wasn't anyone's fault. And trust me—I've tried over and over again to figure out what I could have done differently to keep my baby. There wasn't anything we could have done. It just wasn't time for me to be a mom yet."

"You're going to make a good one." Hope's words were mumbled in Faith's shoulder.

"Thanks." Faith leaned back. "Sam pointed out the other day that even though God didn't want the bad to happen that has hit us lately, we can use it to show the world that life is better with God in your life, even when there are more downs than ups. I'm trying to make sure my blog is showing that. When I first started it, it was just a vent for me, a way to throw my thoughts out to the world and see if anyone cared. But now I can't look at it like that anymore. It's still about me, but it's more importantly about my God, and how you have to hold on to your faith even when the going gets tough—really tough."

"I just kept thinking, what if I hadn't come this summer and added all this stress ..."

"No, Hope. The doctor said the baby never would have made it even if I had carried it longer. It wasn't you. I promise." Faith squeezed her sister again.

"It sounds like you're doing better at conquering your name than I am with mine." Hope frowned.

"I've been working at it for several years now. I thought I had a pretty strong faith before we started trying to get pregnant. But God has shown me that I had very little faith at all. It's much stronger now. But not perfect. I still have to work at it. Just like you'll have to keep working to hold on to your hope."

"Pray for me, Faith." Hope leaned over onto Faith's shoulder. "It's brutal to have so many major decisions at once."

"I've been praying for you, Hope." Faith kissed Hope's head. "It's what big sisters do."

CHAPTER 28

HOPE

When Hope had started camp at the beginning of summer, the last week of July was supposed to be her last one. Instead, she was now thinking she would have at least one more week, if not two. She stared at the calendar on the wall of the office and tried to figure out if she should go ahead and say she could work the last week or not.

"Counting days?" Maria asked from behind her.

Hope turned with a grin. "Trying to figure out if I should say I can work the last week or not. I know a lot of the counselors will be gone by then, but I really have no idea."

"Did they call about the job?" Maria asked.

Hope pulled her phone out of the cubby in the wall. "Actually, I do have a missed call. Let me go check this real quick."

She stepped outside and around to the back of the building. With a swipe of her finger, she dialed her voicemail and waited as it rang. After the voice said she had one new message, she heard, "Hope, this is Ms. Waverly. We spoke at the job fair a couple of weeks ago, and I was wanting to touch base with you to see if you are still interested in a job for this fall. We have a high school math position open, and

I'd love to discuss the possibility of you joining our faculty next month. Please give me a call back ..."

Hope's mind whirled as she listened to the phone number the principal had left. It was from Sam's school. She wondered if he knew about it, or if he would be okay with her teaching in the same school where he taught. She shook her head. What was she thinking? Wasn't she considering giving up teaching and moving to Central America?

She heard the buses start to pull in out front and quickly ended her call. She dropped the phone back in the office but didn't stop to answer Maria's question from earlier. Instead, she dove right into her camp day and tried not to think about the voicemail she had just listened to. She made it halfway through the day before things slowed down. Hope and Joe sat in their cubby and opened pudding packs and soda cans for lunch.

"What's up?" Joe ripped open a packet of ketchup for a boy and then handed it back.

"What do you mean?" She bit into her peanut butter sandwich.

"You've been acting like there's something you don't want to tell me all day long." He tossed a chip at her.

She glanced over at him and sighed. "Can we talk tonight?"

"That doesn't sound promising." He turned to her and leaned down to look into her face. "Is something wrong?"

"No." She motioned around them. "Just need to talk some things over with you without fifteen sets of ears listening in."

He glanced around their space and smiled. "I guess I see what you mean. Pick you up at six-thirty?"

She nodded and returned to eating her sandwich between telling boys to quit playing and finish eating their lunch. The afternoon dragged by even though they stayed as busy as ever. She was glad when Joe left to go drive his bus and she didn't have to see him looking so worried anymore.

"You okay?" Maria asked as Hope waited for the last bus to pull away.

"Just have a lot on my mind." Hope hoped the answer would be good enough to avoid further questions.

"I'm praying for you and Joe. He told me what he asked you the other day. It's a lot. Too sudden," Maria said in a scolding voice. "Don't get me wrong, I'd love to have you as a daughter. But I think he's forcing you into something you aren't ready for yet."

Hope leaned into Maria's hug. "I love him."

"I know you do." Maria squeezed her tight enough she couldn't catch her breath for a moment.

∼

JOE SHOWED up early and chatted with Sam while Hope finished getting ready. She never could get used to the fact that she still felt hot and sticky even after taking a shower. She wouldn't miss that part of camp, for sure. She ran a brush through her hair one more time and headed down the hallway to meet him.

His eyes spoke his approval as he watched her walk into the living room. She hadn't dressed in anything too fancy but had changed into capris and a peasant-style blouse. Her hot pink toenails peeked through her flip flops.

"Ready?" She grabbed her purse.

"Sure." He offered his elbow like a true gentleman.

He took her to an Italian restaurant and opened the door for her. She sat across the booth from him, looking at the menu but not really paying any attention to it. She still wasn't sure what to do, but she needed to let the school know an answer in the next day or two. The waiter interrupted her thoughts and took her order and then her menu. She now had nothing to distract her from the reason she had asked for this dinner.

"Spill it." Joe crossed his arms. "Your fidgeting is driving me crazy. Just get it over with."

"I got a call today."

"Oh?" He shifted. "Which school decided that you really are as good a teacher as you said you were?"

"How did you know?" She crossed her own arms.

"You were avoiding me all day." He pointed at her. "I knew it had something to do with what's up in the air between us. And I figured it was about time for those schools to start getting back with you and maybe even start a bidding war as to which one of them deserves you the most."

"Joe—"

He took both of her hands in his. "I'm not going to force you to give in to me just to make me happy, Hope. I want you to be happy, too. And I know you love teaching."

"But I don't want to leave you." She wanted to stomp her feet at the total unfairness of everything. "And it isn't even one of the schools I'm most interested in. It's the one Sam teaches at. They don't pay as much, and I never felt my calling was to be in a Christian school. So why is this so hard?"

The waiter brought their salads, and they paused until he left again.

Joe picked right back up on the last question she had asked. "Because I haven't made it easy for you. I suggested it but haven't helped work out any of the problems you pointed out would come with such a decision. I just grasped the first idea that popped in my head that I thought would keep us together without thinking it all the way through."

"But it's not such a bad idea, Joe. It just has a lot of things to work out." Hope pushed an onion to the side of her bowl.

They were fairly quiet the rest of the meal, chatting about inconsequential things. After he had paid the check and they were back in the car, he drove south. She sat back and didn't complain. She wasn't ready for this evening to be over yet, either.

They made it just in time to see the bats fly out. She watched them with awe once more. They had found the rock from the week before and reclaimed it for this evening. He held her hand as they watched God's amazing creation displayed before them.

"You'd be good for the school." Joe broke their silence.

"What about you? How will one person replace a family on that mission team?"

"I don't know." He shook his head. "But that was the original plan, so it's not like I'm changing anything. And there will still be three other families. This fall is more about getting me acclimated."

"You might not be changing any of those plans, but you changed me." She squeezed his arm.

He looked at her. She could barely make out his features in the dim lighting, but she thought he looked surprised.

"You were right. I didn't want to hope. I didn't want to believe anything good could happen. But you happened. And you're definitely the best thing in my life right now."

"I thought the guy was supposed to say all the romantic lines and sweep the girl off her feet." He nudged her with his shoulder. "Here you are sweeping me off of mine."

"I like romantic lines as much as the next girl." She ducked her head. "But you needed to know that I have been listening to you."

"A guy always likes to know he's right about something." He grinned.

After a moment, Hope leaned in close to him and whispered, "Know what I told your mom today?"

He shook his head.

"I love you."

She wasn't sure, but she thought maybe he had quit breathing. He took a deep lungful and squeezed her hand tighter in his. Then, he shook his head and gave a little laugh.

"You told my mom you love her?" His voice sounded like he was trying to joke, but not quite making it.

"I told her I love *you*." Hope said it right in his ear.

"How come she got to find out before I did?"

She pushed away from him. "Oh, Joe."

"That's pretty serious stuff." He pulled her back in close. "Especially since I love you, too."

She accepted the kiss he placed on her lips and then leaned back. "That sounds wonderful."

"I think I loved you from the first day I saw you. You looked so lost—and so put out with everything."

"And I had no idea what to do with you." She laughed.

"Do you now?"

"I'm still working it out." She shook her head.

"Hmm." He hopped up and offered her his hand. "Come on. Let's head back to the car. It's getting late."

He didn't start the vehicle right away but turned and looked at her. "So, when you say you love me, does that mean you're also considering going to Honduras with me this fall?"

She gave him as serious a look as she could muster. "You haven't actually asked me properly, you know."

At first, he looked like he wasn't sure what she was talking about. Then, he nodded and held up a finger. He got out, dashed around the vehicle, and opened her door. From deep in his pocket, he pulled something out that caught the streetlight and sparkled.

"Hope, I have loved spending every day of this summer with you." He brushed her cheek with his fingers. "You amazed me with your strength as you dealt with the scrapes and bruises."

His hand traced the scars on her shoulder from her kickball injury earlier in the summer.

"You impressed me with your ability to handle the chaos of fifteen boys all freaking out in a thunderstorm. You astonished me with your amazing cha-cha skills."

She burst out in giggles at that one.

"I can't imagine my life without you in it every day." He knelt, took her hand in his, and slid a diamond ring on her finger. "Will you marry me?"

"I can't imagine my life without you in it every day, either, Joe." A few tears slipped down her cheek. "I'd love to marry you."

He tried to wrap her in a hug, but the seatbelt got in the way. With a frustrated groan, he fiddled with the buckle until it released and pulled her out of the car so he could spin her around in a real hug. She grinned at him when he placed her on the ground again. He leaned in and kissed her sweetly before helping her back in the car.

"I have no idea how all this is going to work." She studied the sparkles on her finger all the way home. Home. When had she started thinking of this place as home?

"It will." He pulled her hand to his lips and gave it a quick kiss. "We just have to start making our plans. And the first one is that you'll call all the schools and tell them you don't need their job after all."

She shook her head. Never in a million years would she have thought at the beginning of the summer that she would be turning down teaching jobs. Now, she couldn't imagine taking one for this fall. She was going to Honduras. With Joe.

EPILOGUE

Early October

Faith hugged Hope one more time before she and Joe would head through security. "Let me know you get there safely, as soon as you can."

"Of course." Hope nodded and repeated the plan one more time. "We're only going down for a few months this time, to make sure I'm certain I want to do this. We'll be back at Christmas." After many long talks with everyone in the family, Hope and Joe had decided not to try to do everything at once. Instead, Hope would stay with one of the other families down there while Joe stayed with the family that would be leaving. That family had decided to stay until the spring. Hope and Joe would learn everything that would be expected of them and see if it was something they wanted long-term.

Hope had agreed that this was a much better plan than marrying in a hurry and starting their new life together by uprooting from everything they had known. Instead, they'd come back in the winter and finish planning the wedding. The church here had promised they would keep the associate minister position open for Joe as long as he wanted it. And Hope had agreed to be a substitute at Sam's school in the spring. Just like Joe had promised, everything was working out.

"It just feels so far away." Faith wrinkled her nose.

"I'll be back before you know it, and we'll be neck-deep in wedding plans. And we'll still be praying for you guys. I want to know as soon as possible when it's time for me to come meet my new niece or nephew."

"I'm not even pregnant yet." Faith nudged Hope's shoulder. "Give a girl time."

"But you're trying again. And that's a step in the right direction." Hope poked her back. "And it will happen. Someday, you're going to be a fabulous mom, and I'll be the child's favorite aunt."

Faith shook her head. "You're nuts."

"Keep the faith, Faith." Hope winked.

"Never give up hope, Hope." Faith widened her eyes.

"And always remember that the greatest of these is love." They fell into a giggly hug.

They attracted quite a bit of attention from the other people hurrying around them, all headed to various destinations and journeys. But Faith and Hope didn't care. It was too nice to be able to laugh and smile again … and to have a sister to love and grow with.

FROM THE AUTHOR

Dear Reader,

Thank you for taking the time to read my book. This story is near and dear to my heart. My husband and I were in the middle of our struggle with infertility when I wrote it. Several friends have mentioned that they wish I had ended the story with Faith already pregnant. I couldn't do that.

At the time this was written, I wasn't sure I was going to get that ending. I also know several amazing couples who never got to have that ending, either. Some adopted. Others are using their lives to serve God in a different way. I wanted to leave you with hope, but also let you use your imagination as to where Faith's story goes from here. Every person who goes through the battle has a slightly different ending. None are wrong. And all can get through it because of the love of God.

My husband and I could have let the stress and frustration and sadness tear us away from each other and God. Instead, we used it to grow closer and stronger. If you're going through this, hang in there. Remember God's faithfulness. And let your friends and family love you through it. If you need someone to listen, please contact me. I'd love to pray for you.

If you enjoyed this story, I'd love for you to share it with a friend. Also, if you can, please leave a review. Reviews, even short ones, help authors by not only lifting our spirits, but also letting others know that people think our story is worth reading. I appreciate it so much.

If you'd like to keep up with me, feel free to check out my website at http://abitofanguish.weebly.com or facebook.com/amyanguishauthor

May you grow in faith, hope, & love.

Amy

ALSO FROM MANTLE ROCK
PUBLISHING

Cheryl Richardson doesn't know that her landlord who owns the other half of the duplex where she lives is plotting to build a bomb—but the FBI does. In order to discover what her landlord is planning to blow up, agent Steve Gableman moves next door to get closer to Cheryl to learn what she knows, namely the target and motive, so they can stop it. But when Steve involves himself in every area of her life, including her dog, will Cheryl be the one to explode?

The Other Neighbor by Gail Sattler.

First-year Special Education teacher Charly Livingston demonstrates God's love on the outside but is resentful that God allowed back-to-back tragedies in her family.

Rance Butler is a top-notch medical intern. He's on his way to the top, and when he meets Charly, he knows things will only get better. When he discovers family secrets and a dying father he never knew, his easy, carefree life seems to disintegrate.

Even in the idyllic ocean breezes and South Carolina sunshine, contentment turns to bitterness and confusion except for God's amazing grace.

Carolina Grace, the third book in the Southern Breeze Series by Regina Rudd Merrick.

MANTLE ROCK PUBLISHING LLC

Stay up-to-date on your favorite books and authors with our free e-newsletters.
mantlerockpublishingllc.com

facebook.com/mantlerockpbulishing

Made in the USA
Lexington, KY
15 April 2019